PIP OF
SEDRO WOOLLEY

PIP OF
SEDRO WOOLLEY

an illustrated novel

Ruta Sevo

First Printing August 2019

ISBN 978-0-9991187-5-7

Momox Publishing
Contact: ruta@momox.org
www.momox.org

Available as a Kindle ebook or paperback online

A work of fiction. All people and events are imaginary.

"See us cuddle and hug," say the Pleiades,

"All six in a ring: it keeps us warm:

We huddle together like birds in a storm:

It's bitter weather tonight."

Robert Graves (1895–1985) Star Talk

"What we think is impossible is in fact possible."

Mary Rodwell, Awakening, p. 271

"The Universe is entirely mental. ... The Universe is immaterial--mental and spiritual. ... Nothing exists but observations."

Richard Conn Henry, "The mental
universe" in NATURE, vol 436/7, July 2005

"The very strength of our resistance to the evidence on UFOs suggests to me that there is clearly a phenomenon of surpassing importance here."

Dr. Robert L. Hall, Professor of Sociology,
University of Illinois (paper presented to the
American Association for the Advancement of
Science, 1969)

"Reality is merely an illusion. ... The distinction between the past, present and future is only a stubbornly persistent illusion."

Albert Einstein

TABLE OF CONTENTS

PART ONE: NEED TO RISE

A Departure

Esme CAME DOWN FOR BREAKFAST and saw her mother crumpled over the dining table, crying her eyes out. "Caroline's dead! I don't believe it!"

Now tears flooded her eyes too. "What happened?" Caroline was her godmother and practically a member of the family.

"Somebody called the police and said to go check her house." Molly was still in her dark-green terry-cloth robe, her shoulder-length blond hair disheveled from sleep. The phone was face down on the table. She didn't look like she could move.

"So, they're on their way there?" asked Esme.

"Yes. I assume."

Esme ran to the stairs and called up: "Simon! Simon! Come on!" There was no time to lose. She knew there was something at Caroline's house that couldn't stay there. Caroline had another role in Esme's life: she was the leader of their secret group, and, most important right now, the guardian of a precious object.

They grabbed their summer jackets.

"We'll go over there, Mom," said Esme.

"Don't get in the way, my dears. I'll call the police and whoever, too, and try to help them sort things out." Molly sounded like she didn't believe there was a crime involved. Something had made Caroline go. She was healthy two days ago. "We can't bring her back. Her things are nothing. Even her body. You know her heart is with us." She choked.

"I'm sorry, Mom." Esme dumped her cereal bowl in the sink. She went over to Molly and hugged her. "You just chill. One day at a time." Esme was only twelve, but she'd been around Caroline and Molly so long that she sounded like them when she was nurturing.

They pedaled their bikes as hard as they could to beat the police to Caroline's house, only a mile away, but they were too late. There were four police cars clustered in front of her godmother's house, willy-nilly, as if there'd been a shoot-out.

When they saw the police, they got off and walked their bikes down the middle of the gravel road, slowly, as if they were just passing through.

Esme kept her voice low. "Remember we've got to stay invisible," she said to Simon. "That's the most important thing. Off the radar."

Then, as if talking to herself: "We have to play a long game. We could be set back centuries. We do NOT want them to 'get to know us.' Quite the opposite."

She looked straight at Simon to make sure he was listening. He was only ten. You couldn't always count on him to listen. Sage Sherman had taught her, and now she needed to coach Simon. One way to coach him was to think out loud.

It was mid-afternoon, and overcast. You could feel the perpetual Mist of the Northwest in the air, letting a few drops form now and then, carrying the smell of wet evergreen. Greenery everywhere was dewy but not dripping.

They stopped just as Officer Kameron waved them to stay away. He was tying police tape across the chain link fence in

4

front of the house, because any minute, reporters might arrive, from Seattle or Bellingham.

"You kids don't need to stop here," he said, with forced modulation. His belly looked swollen under his shirt. The sloppy bulge was inconsistent with the authority of the uniform; he was not in control of that bulge. His shirt tails were uncomfortably shoved into his pants, also too tight. It wasn't often a group of police were called for, in this neck of the world. Their team had shown up "all out."

"Okay, Sir," said Esme, remembering Sherman's advice. Low profile. It wasn't every day that Kameron was called "sir." She knew that.

"Stay over on the other side of the road. There'll be cars pulling up any minute. Watch out." He smiled, putting on the gentle face he used around kids in school. He seemed to be trying not to come on strong.

"We will, Mr. Kameron." Esme knew him from his visits at school, talking about safety.

She was light-brown, with sloppy reddish-black hair, a dirty painter's hat, untucked plaid shirt, jeans, and sneakers that hadn't seen a wash in many muddy months. Kind people would call her cute, but she preferred unremarkable.

Simon on the other hand was tall and heading toward worry as a boy with a will. Only ten, he had the tousled hair of a little boy, but his body was moving with muscular assertion. Rock climbing had trained him to move with deliberate, precise movements, unafraid. The balance of his lean body was, yes, remarkable.

Nothing had happened, yet, to make them aware of being biracial.

Many eons in the past and many eons in the future, and well, really in the no-time and no-space of the universe, and in the now, a soul group of Pleiadians chose to reincarnate on Earth, and come to live in Sedro Woolley, as part of their soul-healing mission. Their bodies are light energy but in Earthly form they take the shape of star-seeds: humans and animals with slightly modified DNA. In this way they are like missionaries who "go native" but have an additional agenda, which is to help humans evolve to a higher dimension and to prevent the destruction of the Earth.

Thus, Simon was born into Esme's family two years after her, and they recognized each other, and started to recognize other Pleiadians, especially when Caroline found them and various animals in Sedro Woolley.

Although Esme treated Simon like an apprentice, they both knew that they'd go into the future as peers, eventually. They'd been allies from the git-go. As a big sister on Earth, Esme appreciated the playmate, and the trainee in him, as soon as he'd arrived. He appreciated that he was allowed to do a lot of things because Esme was there to help him and protect him. She didn't pull power plays on him, like a typical older sibling, making him do humiliating things to remind him that he was the second kid. In fact, she'd been possessive and protective of him since she was two years old. Their parents trusted her with him. For Simon, she was adventurous, fun to follow, and a natural body guard, which, it turns out, he needed.

His windbreaker said "Windhill Horse Rescue" in white letters on navy pseudo-satin. His mom had picked it up used. He wore shabby, high-end canvas climbing shoes. Their family thrived on the fringes of richer people and their stuff.

The kids watched an old, blue, dirty Honda civic pull up and deliver two people, a girl and a guy in their early twenties. If they were reporters, they were as junior as you could be. It was an hour's drive from Seattle, or half an hour from Bellingham, a gloomy day in August. The two barely glanced at the kids, heading for the Officer.

"Hey there," the guy said to Kameron, "Seattle Times. We're here for the story."

"Fine. Expecting you. We're roped off in case we get a crowd. You're the first."

"Super," said the guy. He pulled out a smart phone and spoke into it. "Sedro Woolley. August 15th. Dead person in a farm house."

He turned to Kameron. "What happened?"

"Well," said Officer Kameron, seeming reluctant to give a long speech to just two people. "We got a call that the resident lady, Caroline Milarep, needed to be checked on. When the first officer got here, he found that she was gone, probably deceased."

"What do you mean 'probably?'" asked the girl.

"There were remains in one of the rooms."

"Remains? You mean her body?"

"No, ma'am. I mean remains. A pile of ashes, with a few bits indicating it had been a body."

7

"Wow. Wait." The two looked quite alert, now. "What bits are we talking about?"

"Nails. Teeth. What might be left in a cremation situation."

Esme had never actually seen cremation remains, and had no frame of reference for what he said. She looked at Simon, hoping that he wasn't tempted to jump in with his own questions.

Kameron continued, "Something like the finest gray dust you might empty from a barbecue grill, only inside the dust were clearly human parts. The small amount of dust wasn't even hot. One breath would disturb most of it."

"There was a fire?"

"No. No fire."

"How do you explain that?"

"Well," Kameron took a step back, defensively. "We don't yet. Never seen it before. Our people are taking photos and samples now."

"And who called you?"

"We don't know. Anonymous phone call. Last night. Could've been a neighbor. They weren't upset. Just matter of fact. Like we shouldn't leave the house empty, as it seemed to be."

Arrggh, thought Esme. If they'd just held off. Was it somebody just trying to be helpful? Or, a grumpy neighbor. Somebody who watched Caroline, looking for something to report. Something that might make them feel that they just had to do something about her. Sound the alarm.

Or, a new client. Some unsuspecting lady, blundering into a shocking discovery. Maybe not finding her home when they were scheduled to see her.

Caroline had visitors coming to her house from all over, for psychic consultations and healing. Services that anybody in Seattle wouldn't blink at, but in Sedro Woolley, they used the word "witch." Might be. Not your usual down-and-out old lady with a colorful past that probably involved a drunken husband, lost jobs, scrapping by with minimum-wage jobs into her old age, barely still on her feet.

In fact, if she had just been the usual drunk and poor, they would have found her boring. Like a lot of other people. That kind of person was understandable. Although among them, in Sedro Woolley, were other colorful types. Early on, homesteaders looking for work with the lumber yards and railway. Mental hospital staff and "graduated" patients, many who were first- and second-generation immigrants. Hippies who'd migrated North from Haight-Ashbury fifty years ago, to Oregon and Western Washington, and then they had children, and who knows what those kids turned into. Caroline was very New Age, with flowing shirts and skirts, and quite presentable, not scruffy. She made it hard for busy-bodies to label her dangerous.

Officer Kameron continued to brief the reporters. It was a poor media turnout. Seattle folks probably scratched their heads when they got the lead. People died in Sedro Woolley all the time, and it was rarely newsworthy. It was another rural area off everyone's radar. Sleepy. Woody. Many working class, poor people. Old mountaineers settling into the foothills of Mt. Baker. Drop-outs who didn't want a nine-to-five job, just piece work. People who lived on disability and unemployment benefits, or a green harvest from Las Vegas. You could get by, in Sedro Woolley, with an RV and a truck. Silly stereotypes stuck, while the population was shifting to people who were building million-dollar homes and using the place as a bedroom community, commuting to Seattle for work.

Esme knew Caroline's house as if it were her own. She recoiled at the thought of curious strangers traipsing through its back rooms. A violation, really.

"I sure hope she's gone," she said to Simon. "This is like an autopsy. These people are looking for crazy, strange. She would've opened her door for them, and now they can just walk in."

"Esme," Simon adjusted his grip on the handlebars, as if a thought had woken his body, "She's invited them in, in any case. You know she wouldn't mind."

"You're right. Another way to make'em think, I guess."

The house was small but pretty. It had a Swedish look, wood painted dark red and tidy windows. Caroline wasn't poor, and she took care of it. The trim around windows and doors had been painted a clean white. The windows were washed. The porch swept. No broken banisters or rails. The yard was wild grass but tamed to provide a pretty soft carpet up to the fence. It was not a psychic's haven with wind chimes, Tibetan flags, and butterfly lawn ornaments. In fact, Caroline's life was fairly austere: she'd said she preferred a rich inner life to a flashy, cluttered space.

The reporters turned to the kids with their bikes.

"Did you know Mrs. Milarep?" one asked.

"Not really," said Simon with a straight, know-nothing face.

The reporters were quick to give up. Just kids. Gawking.
They turned to walk away.

"Drat. We have a problem," Esme said under her breath.

A little article in the Seattle Times used the word "mystery" in the title. It said the police did not suspect foul play, because they found a note, blatantly left on the kitchen table. It said, "Hello, to whom it may concern. Welcome to my house. I am indeed gone. Please be gentle with my property." Also, on the note was something that no one could decipher, so the newspaper printed it and asked for help:

हमारा शरीर प्रकाश है , हम अमर हैं।
हमारा शरीर चार है , हम अनन्त हैं।

According to the article, the handling of Caroline's property was turned over to the Office of Social Services, who would look for the next of kin, and a will.

An Emergency

THAT EVENING AFTER DINNER, Esme and Simon went upstairs to her room, as they usually did, to read or play before bedtime. Molly stayed in the living room, sitting by the fire wrapped in a wool blanket (on the August night), drinking a hot toddy with their dad, Donald. The parents were exhausted, processing every aspect of Caroline's demise. They'd talked to friends all day, by phone and in person.

Esme sent her thoughts to the large black cat on her bed: *Penelope, you need to let everybody know. Marker 369 XC in the Bug House cemetery. Ten a.m.* ("Bug House" is slang for an insane asylum.)

She turned to Simon. "Do you think that's enough time?"

"I think so. We can't afford to wait too long." He didn't sound sure, but had a hint of hope. He was picking up Esme's assertive tone of voice.

Their other cat, a Russian blue named Persephone, was nestled on Esme's pillow. (The cats were adopted during the family's Greek mythology phase.) Persephone's job was not to be a messenger, but to be a comfort to others. She didn't really like night rounds -- too much going on, out there. She liked to hang close to the house, purring to set the atmosphere as much as she had energy. Like a heart warmer. She assigned herself the job of being a calming presence to offset rough vibrations in the surroundings, of which there seemed an endless supply.

Esme made sure the window was open. Penelope eagerly leaped to the window seat and disappeared through the opening like a UFO disappearing in the sky. Ha ha.

Their little schnoodle (schnauzer-poodle) Pip had settled into an actual dog bed near the door. (He was named during their Charles Dickens phase.) He was not a night runner, but Molly would be letting him out the door as early as 6 a.m., and then he would make his rounds. Their yard had no dog-proof fence, and Molly knew Pip would not run off to get away from them. The risk was somebody wanting to dog-nap him, because he was terminally cute: giant stand-up ears, 12 pounder, short black hair/fur with the brains of a poodle and the heart of a schnauzer. Pip knew the risks, and behaved more like a fox than a dog when he was "out there." In fact, he passed the baton to Harold the fox as soon as he could. People assumed a cute lap dog in the middle of the woods was most certainly lost.

Penelope immediately found her nearest partner, a Calico cat, in an alley known to have a colony of mice. The cat immediately dropped his favorite hobby, which was observing mice, realizing the urgency of the mission. He took off to cover his territories. Between them, they reached Carl-Crow, found tearing up a black garbage bag behind a restaurant in the early morning, and another hound dog. A fox came out of his den to

Carl's cawing. Sherman, another hound dog, already knew. Somehow, he always knew things nobody had told him.

Penelope dropped a dog toy at John the Farmer's door step. (She didn't want to use up one of her own cat toys, so one of Pip's hoard of shredded stuffed animals was sacrificed to the cause.) She encoded a thought message, in case John's thick human head was not awake enough to pick up the news. They

didn't actually want John to show up. He would be the only adult there if he did. He was "on call" in case larger human capabilities were needed, like a truck. It was an "FYI." The minute he picked up the thing on his doorstep and it made contact with his body, it gave him the message directly to his mind.

The next morning, Penelope-the-black-cat was the first to arrive at marker 369 XC. She raised her black tail high as a signal for the others. It was early on a sunny day, so little creatures had to navigate dewy grasses.

"369 XC" stood for Xavier Corona, patient number 369 to be buried in the cemetery on the campus of the old Northern State Hospital. The cemetery was on the fringes of the compound, and their selected meeting place was near woods, for quick passage onto the field and back. About 1500 patients had been buried this way--marked by a simple stone, because there were so many, and the hospital wasn't going to invest in monuments for anonymous burials. If no family came to pick up the body, then this was the beggar's field. It was large from the spread of fifty years' burials.

Dead patients weren't the only "lost souls" at the Bug House. Many of the doctors were displaced persons who had escaped the Nazi's in Europe. They could work in a mental hospital and try to re-qualify for general medical practice in America and recover their lost professional life and social status. There were many single nurses who saw a chance to apprentice there (since it was a premier learning center for psychiatric care), but had to find a social life in this isolated outpost by sneaking out and driving to dance halls in Mount Vernon. A network of tunnels made that possible. There had been a locked-down ward for the criminally insane.

Among the patients were post-menopausal women, committed by hostile husbands, orphans put into temporary care because there was no other place for them, and emergency admissions from crime scenes. Prisoners. Many forgotten, in life or death, and, if they were even more unlucky, they suffered violence at the hands of staff who were not all that healthy themselves.

The Pleiadians found the place a sanctuary. The place's history of marginalized people, crazy people, people isolated from normal society, worked to frighten visitors. Or fascinate them from a distance. Although it was a campus of abandoned buildings, the Bug House was notorious for ghosts. Pleiadians were not normal, either.

"There you are!" shouted Esme as she made her way out of the woods. She leaned down to pet Penelope-the-black-cat although it seemed a very false gesture, typical of humans, of some kind of dominance, but she meant it as a hand-shake. Penelope understood, and she sat down, now that the height of Esme made their location visible and her tall tail was not needed.

Soon Sherman the hound dog, another cat, another hound dog, Carl-Crow, and Pip-the-schnoodle were gathered. Simon stood with his hands in his jeans pockets, concerned.

"Here's the problem," started Esme. "Caroline was keeping The Find in a box in her shed. We have to get to it before the police or Social Services go in there."

Why don't we just go over there now and get it? thought Pip, which everyone could "hear."

"We don't want to attract any attention. That's the trick," said Esme.

Stay off the radar, thought Sherman. *Much is at stake.* He never looked concerned. He never raised excitement, because creatures did not think clearly if they triggered their fight-and-flight hormones. True, they all indeed had animal brains, here, and this had to be managed, when occupying such primitive vehicles as a mammal's body.

How big is the box? I know there's an entry hole just below the front porch. The Calico cat knew that all the mice had little entry-

17

ways into the sheds, although they respected the "no poop" rule so they could scout for crumbs without detection. The mice also played a long game.

"Shoebox size. Metal. An old lunch box," said Simon. He collected old cigar boxes for his rock collections and was quite aware of containers in that size range.

"Can we get somebody to make the entry bigger?" Esme looked around. Who had good teeth?

"We could break a window," offered Simon. He looked at Esme, who'd spent more time in the shed with Caroline.

"Well, it has a lot of big windows. But what about the noise?"

Well Esme, Sherman said, *did she keep it locked?*

"Yes, exactly because The Find is in there. There are meditation things--the singing bowl, crystals, a nice Tibetan mat. It's almost bare."

You're the most capable of picking it up and running with it, noted Bailey-the-hound-dog, who was usually off in his head thinking something through and then jumping into the conversation. *We'd best get you in there, or Junior, here,* pointing to Simon.

I saw this once, Esme. You put duct tape on the window, a pillow over the window, and a blanket or pillow under it. Then hit it with a rock. That muffles the sound. The Calico was smug.

"That's a plan. See you tonight, people. Ten-ish." Esme looked around for agreement.

"Off we go!" Simon said, a little too loudly. He couldn't help himself. He loved an adventure!

As they traipsed through the woods heading home, Simon asked, "Esme, why did Caroline leave it behind? Why did she risk it?"

"I don't know." The question had bothered Esme too. "Maybe she couldn't take it with her. Maybe that's something we need to ask her spirit when we get a chance."

Caroline had told them about the box a year ago. They'd never seen the contents, but "it" was something that Caroline found on one of her mystery night hikes. She said she'd been guided to it, and instructed to protect it. She said there were Earthly "authorities" who would make a big deal of it. It could reveal something so scary that people who knew about it would need to be "contained." She told them, "Imagine when early humans saw their first solar eclipse and thought the sun had disappeared from the sky. That scary."

Did Caroline figure they would protect it? That they could protect it?

They couldn't help but look in the direction of the Hospital. They could see a few people on the grounds outside, in the

distance. The place attracted ghost hunters who had sensitive equipment to capture fragments of eerie sounds that they took to be the spoken words of ghosts. There were also hikers who came to the old campus, not deterred by the creepy atmosphere surrounding the place after it closed in 1973, after being a mental hospital for sixty years. The place had been like a small, self-sufficient community, maintained by the labor of over a thousand patients at any given time. It was like an intentional community of the 60s except the intention here was the containment, and hopefully healing, of the insane.

Mission

"MOM, WE'RE GOING OUT to hunt bats," Esme shouted over her shoulder as she pushed Simon out the door into the darkness. It was after sundown but before bedtime. Molly strongly believed in the independence of children, even at night.

Esme was carrying two old floppy down pillows, formerly used as dog beds, in her arms. Simon had a large roll of wide masking tape in his khaki canvas backpack. Both wore camping headlamps.

"Bat hunting" meant going to intersections where street lights showed bats flying overhead, and you threw socks with some rocks in them up in the air, making the bat dive for it. All the kids thought bats would knock themselves out. Also, that bats would miss, swoop into your hair, get tangled, and bite you. It hadn't happened yet, ever, but you know. Lots of screams in mock and real terror.

They hiked in single file away from the house, with Pip following, into paths through the woods in back, over to the back of Caroline's house.

They turned off their headlamps about fifty feet before arrival, so that no one would see any activity near the house. Next to the house they could see, if they opened their eyes to the dark, the shapes of a fellow Pleiadians.

Esme pulled an old wooden crate up to a back window, which was as large as four feet tall and two feet wide. Caroline had designed her she-shed to let in a lot of light. There were tall windows on three sides, and one next to the front door. Because she'd used a pad-lock, there was no sense going through the front window to open any kind of latch. The front was more exposed to the street. They needed to climb through in back of the shed.

Esme stood on the crate. "Hand me the tape, Simon," she whispered. She taped the glass.

"Okay. Simon, hand me a rock."

She placed on pillow on the glass and the other at her feet to catch shards. "Calico, Pip. You go to the front, ready to make noise. When you hear me hit the glass, go for it. Keep it up for a few minutes, because I may have to hit it a few times."

The street was still much further away in front of the main house. Neighbors were even further than that.

"Ready, guys?"

Ready. said Sherman.

She held the rock with its sharpest corner facing out. At Easter, they had a tradition of hitting the tips of eggs against each other, and she'd arrived at her own technique: a short, precise smack.

She smacked the pane in the middle. Nothing. Hardly loud and inconsequential. Harder smack! It made noise.

They heard a cat and a dog get into a loud fight nearby. The cat howling, hissing. The dog barking in a high pitch, hysterical. A commotion you might hear if a raccoon had surprised two animals, which is unlikely because the two would have surprised each other already if they were that close together. Dogs and cats in cahoots. Not usual.

Another smack and the glass broke. Some shards fell down in front of her. Most fell into the room. She quickly smacked in a circle around the first hole, with sections of glass falling in sheets.

"Simon, are you ready?"

The two climbed through the window.

An L-shaped platform filled nearly all of the back and half of one side. Their entry was onto a mattress on the platform. Which was now a bed of broken glass, in the dark.

Esme took her headlamp into her hand and switched it on, blocking most of the light. They could see the outlines of the room. One corner was all triangular built-in shelves. A table near them held Caroline's "temple" pieces: small bowls for water and oil lamps, candles, a tiny primitive stone Buddha made from lava rock, a rustic wooden incense holder, and a medium-sized Tibetan singing bowl with its plain wooden mallet. Incense sticks. Caroline was a minimalist. No giant silk mandala. No artificial flowers. No Himalayan salt lamp. Anyway, there was

23

no electricity to the shed. Any light for the occupant was candles and battery-operated lamp or flashlight. There was a band of Tibetan prayer flags high across one wall, above the windows.

Esme knelt by the bed and pointed the light coming between her fingers onto a single-row bookshelf that fit under the platform, under its whole length. It was used for storage. The edge of the bedspread from India covering the mattress came down over the bookcase. There were books stacked and shelved there, along with a shoe-box, slippers, a flower vase, a plastic box of writing materials.

"Simon, take hold of the bookshelf at your end. We're going to pull it out."

The two slowly pulled the shelf from under the platform, heavy with its contents. With about two feet of space behind it, she could squeeze back under the platform. She lay on the floor and reached to the far back under the platform.

"Got it," she said.

They pushed the book shelf back into place under the platform. Pulled the orange bedspread back down.

A child's metal lunch-box was passed through the window. It was something Caroline had brought back from India as a souvenir.

The Calico and Pip were still in front of the shed ready to throw another fake brawl if necessary. Bailey-the-hound-dog was sent to call them back.

Simon put the box in his backpack, along with the roll of remaining tape. Esme balled the two pillows, folding the side with shards sides together, and put the bundle under her arm carefully.

The troop made its way single file, in the dark, until they were deep in the woods and there were no houses near.

Well away from Caroline's house, they regrouped.

You don't want that in your house, Esme. said Sherman.

"I know. What now?"

Tibetan Cave. Bailey spoke up. Paused. *On Farmer John's property.*

Nobody ever goes there. Nobody knows about it but us. added Penelope.

"That's a long way," said Simon.

A couple of roads to cross, added Harold.

Big Cedar Hole. said Pip. *For now. It's close enough.*

"Okay. Who's coming?" asked Esme. Simon and Pip followed her.

The Big Cedar Hole was on a triangular vector with Caroline's and Molly's houses. It would take only ten minutes.

The three used headlamps to move quickly through the woods, following deer paths. The Big Cedar Hole was big enough to hold the lunch box. Esme pushed it through the opening at an angle, and then pushed it up out of sight, jamming it up into a stable position. They stuffed branches and organic matter from the forest floor after it. It would be invisible even if some critter dug away some of the mulch.

A Missing Person

THE SEDRO SENTINEL CAME OUT with a featured article, with much more prominence than the one in *The Seattle Times:*

"Where's the Body? Local Death Poses a Puzzle

The police have made a determination that the death of local citizen Caroline Milarep is indeed a case of suicide. There is no evidence   of forced entry into her home. The subject left a note. However, her body has not been found. Only a small pile of finger nails and a few bones were found, which DNA evidence shows to be hers.

The police are at a loss as to what kind of expert they need to consult. Anyone with information is asked to step forward."

No one stepped up as family, nor posted an obituary. After the article was published, there was much town gossip. People who had been her clients were reluctant to admit it, due to the personal nature of their consultations, for example, "Is my husband having an affair?" "Will my addicted nephew die soon?" "Does my boss really hate me and will I get fired?" "Will I find love?" "Is this Mr. Right?" and so on. People felt free to talk about others, however: "My cousin from out of town visited her, but I waited in the car." "I saw a limo with tinted windows and Canadian license plates pull up." "Certain people seem to visit her a lot."

Of course, there were kind words too: "She was a saint." "The sweetest woman you will ever know." "A healer, they say, with a national reputation."

To many, though, it smacked of black magic. Real life was not supposed to be as creepy as horror shows.

The kids were not immune. While they were mostly invisible when they were in public places, they overheard the comments.

"Mom," asked Simon, "Why are they calling Caroline a witch?"

"Because they don't understand the kind of work she did." Molly was best friends with Caroline and knew her as a healer, and a psychic. She'd trusted her kids with a close relationship, regarding it an apprenticeship in healing arts and energy work.

"But what makes them use that word?"

"It's a word people use for someone strange to them. Someone they don't understand."

"They said she did the work of the devil, Mom," said Esme.

"I know. I know. Just ignore them. The important thing is we know who she was, and what she meant to us."

"But I want to hit them," said Simon. Sometimes the human and child part of him overruled the peaceful Pleiadian inside.

"Then you're just like her enemies, Simon. Hitting them doesn't change anybody's mind. You change their mind by acting as an example, an example of love and respect for her."

Esme could remember the day she learned that Caroline was her godmother.

They were having a picnic next to a creek that ran into the Skagit River. It was a grand picnic of favorite foods for kids: tuna fish sandwiches, chocolate chip cookies, bananas, chocolate and sodas instead of juice. Her mom and Caroline were lying in the grass on a small quilt, with backpacks as pillows under their heads. As usual, they were talking and laughing, on and on. Esme and Simon were exploring rocks on the river bank, looking for critters and flat stones, and driftwood shaped like bones.

They were settled near the base of a large tree that had fallen across the creek and made a bridge. It was a great place to climb up, lie face down on the ample trunk, and watch chipmunks that ran up along log and got close before they realized a human was in the way. They hoped a chipmunk mistook them for a friend and came up to them. This was before Esme had met the Cabal and had a lot of animal friends.

Her father Donald was the opposite of protective. He actually encouraged taking risks. It was usually when he was in reach to rescue a little one by grabbing them at the last minute. Anyway, she knew he would look at that tree and say: "See if you can cross that." And she would, suppressing fear in the pit of her stomach. One foot at a time. Try not to look down at the water pouring over rocks, several feet below her.

She was out on the log about five feet over the water, on her stomach, dangling a stick in the water, looking for fish, when she made a mistake. Her hands rushed to grip the deep ridges in the bark of the tree trunk but they were not deep enough to grab, and her hug of the log was not adequate to stop a slide to the side, her fingers fruitlessly scraping the bark as they lost traction and her weight succumbed to gravity. The stick dropped in the water, and there was a four-year-old little girl dropping right after it. She shouted: "Ma!"

The water was only about half a foot deep but swift over rocks, some of which were protruding above the water. It wasn't a sweet beach where you might wade on rocks and find flat places for each step. Also, it was freezing cold, having started from the snows on Mount Baker. Wild, relentless, unforgiving, pounding water.

Esme could feel her hand enter the water in a recess next to a big rock. Her arm sunk to her shoulder. Her face smacked the water and the pain of freezing cold and trauma shot through her body. She immediately got her face above water but the rest of her was like a fish getting rinsed and scrubbed in a processing tank. The water was not going to stop just because she was there.

In nearly the next minute, her other arm was grabbed and pulled up. She was suddenly on her feet, braced against a much larger body that reached over and took up her waist. She was pulled tight into strong human arms, all the way up to the soaking wet neck of Caroline. She was gasping, but with relief. She clung to her rescuer as Caroline slowly found footholds in the creek back to the shore.

They wrapped her in the quilt. Molly carried her all the way home tight against her warm body.

At home, while she sat warm in a bubble bath, Molly said, "You know, Esme, Caroline is your godmother."

"She is? What does that mean?"

"It means she will take care of you when I can't. And when your Dad can't."

"Always? Or just when I'm little?"

"Always. On earth and in spirit."

"Okay."

And now Esme had lost her godmother, on earth at least. It was a terrible feeling. Too big to think about, really. But there were more important things to do than dwell on that, right now. An emergency.

The Cabal

WHEN ESME WAS ONLY FOUR YEARS OLD, Molly often saw her talking to herself. She sat on the floor and dressed dolls, or built little houses for her menagerie of stuffed animals and dolls. There was almost constant chatter. At lunch, Esme pulled the raisins out of her oatmeal, or onions and carrots out of her soup, and placed them in a little pile to the side.

"And who's going to eat that," Molly asked, ready to give a little parental rebuke for wasting food.

"Lulu," said Esme, not looking up.

"Lulu?"

"She likes some stuff that I don't like, so it's okay."

"She likes raisins?" Molly made a face to mock Esme's dislike.

"Especially."

"And what if you eat all of everything?"

"She's good. Just a little treat now and then. She has her own food." Esme pushed the raisins into a neat pile.

"And what else does Lulu eat?"

Esme thought for a minute. "Daisies. And apples. Sometimes apples."

"Does she let you have some?"

"She does. If she's not too hungry."

32

Molly paused, and turned away. "Is she with you in your room?"

"Yes."

Molly turned back. "All the time, or just sometimes?"

"All the time. She sleeps a lot, like the cats." Esme chuckled.

"And what does she look like?"

"She has slightly slanted eyes. Like Chinese. A little."

"And she has her own clothes or does she wear yours?" Molly tugged at Esme's shirt.

Esme laughed out loud. "Oh my gosh she would never fit mine!"

"Why?"

"She's like a skinny fairy. She's got this shiny blue leotard. Like a dance leotard."

"Skinnier than you?"

"For sure. She's little."

"Do we need to do anything for Lulu?" Molly was worried about psychological things going on.

"No. Just let her come and go when she wants to." Esme hummed a little tune and bounced around, illustrating freedom.

"I see." Molly got up and cleared the table. There was a little pile of raisins left on the place mat. She'd read about imaginary friends. The advice was: don't deny them.

Soon after Esme had told Molly about Lulu, she was at Caroline's house, on the platform bed in the she-shed, while Molly ran errands in town for a few hours. Molly shared everything with Caroline, so she'd heard about the conversation.

"I hear you've got a buddy, Esme," Caroline said. "Lulu?"

"Yes."

"Is she here with us?" Like Molly, Caroline sounded casual.

"No. She had to go run errands too."

"I see." Caroline put her book down and leaned over a large cushion, close to the coloring book. "Can you draw her?"

"I'm not so good."

"What if you tell me what to draw?" Caroline picked up a green crayon. As Esme talked, she drew a skinny stick figure with a largish head, slanted eyes, a small mouth, scant brown hair, wearing a leotard and barefoot. She asked about a tutu, but none was called for. Not the cliched princess.

"Does she talk to you?"

"Oh yes. But not with her voice. In her mind."

"Ah. And what does she say?"

"She sings little songs to me. Nonsense. She's fun."

"Does she help you go to sleep?"

"Yes. She's like a cat, really. She curls up and purrs and hums. It makes me feel good."

"Esme, I'm going to tell you something that must be a secret between us."

"Okay."

"All kinds of creatures can talk to you with their minds. Cats, dogs, squirrels, birds. You just have to be prepared to hear them."

"And what do they talk about?" Esme picked up the drawing.

"About helping each other. About having fun together. About being nice to people. Nice to the earth."

"Everybody?"

"No. There are some of us that are here in this world as a secret group. A cabal. You'll know when you hear them in your mind." Caroline put her hand on her arm.

"Like a club."

"Yes." Caroline drew a circle on the paper. She drew a few other overlapping circles. "We are not like ordinary people. We talk across species, like people and animals. And spirits, like Lulu. People in another time called them sylphs -- they are purely nice air spirits."

"Lulu is spirit?"

"Yes. She's probably with you to help you grow up and understand your abilities."

"Like a big sister." Esme nodded.

"Yes. But not a human."

"Oh."

"Soon," said Caroline, "you'll start hearing thoughts from animals around you, and thoughts from some people. You mustn't be surprised. And you should know that all the people around you are not like us."

"Why not?"

"We come from different places. You and I come from the Pleiades, which are planets far away. Soon after we arrive here, we find each other." She paused. "You should know also, that there are people who are afraid of Pleiadians."

"Why are they afraid?"

"Well, they don't believe in life forms or spirits from other planets. They're afraid of extra-terrestrials. Terrestrial means 'of the earth.' We're either hybrids, a combination of earthly and extra-terrestrial, or pure extra-terrestrials."

"What will the earth people do if they find out?" Esme said, matter of fact.

"They might try to hurt us. They might try to take us somewhere and hide us. They're afraid that we want to take over the earth and make humans into slaves."

"Do we?"

"No. We're here to help the planet and humans. We want to make the earth survive some pretty bad things that people -- the pure human types -- do. Some of them kill animals, spoil the water, poison the earth."

"Don't they want to protect the earth too?"

"Some of them do, but many just want to get rich, or have power over others. Humans have some weaknesses. They can be stupid. Mean."

"And we can stop them?"

"We try. That's why we're a cabal. A secret society. We must survive their meanness and their wish to overpower or eliminate us. We're here to help the humans who want the planet to survive, and those who want to take care of people, stop exploiting others. We want to help people who want to help animal species survive even though human civilizations have spoiled their habitats."

"The Pleiades Cabal."

"Yes," said Caroline. "Lulu was sent to make you strong."

Will You Go Before the Gladiators?

THEY ALL KNEW THE STORY of Gloria by heart.

Gloria the elephant was born in a zoo in Kentucky. She was sold before she was one year old, as "excess inventory." A long train ride brought her to the West Coast. She cried for her mom and dad every night, but her handlers had never heard an elephant cry before and they thought that it was just the way elephants sound. Howls of the wild. A few horses and dogs became her best friends.

She grew larger than anyone had imagined and her owners were so frightened of her power that they kept her in chains. Her mammoth body was transported in rail cars and inside large commercial moving trucks, all around the coast to fairs and festivals, for entertainment. She was made to stand on exhibit in the sweltering sun, all day, as families walked by and stared. Children were kept from petting her and feeding her their candied apples, as her handlers were afraid of the hazards of exciting her and any liability.

Finally, one day in Sedro Woolley, Gloria lost it. She broke the flimsy chains on all four legs, flipped her handler a slap in the face with her trunk, and marched freely down Route 20. Miles out of town she arrived at the grounds of the Bug House, which was already an abandoned ghost town by then. There were alarms raised all over the county as police blocked traffic and followed her. When she got to the Bug House, she found Hansen Creek and lumbered into it for a little spa treatment. After a rousing bath and screeching with glee, she lay down on a patch of grass and died.

Humans think animals are dumb, explained Sherman. *They put dogs in crates all day. They incarcerate dolphins and make them perform their whole lives. They keep banks of cages of rabbits, monkeys, and mice to run experiments on their bodies and test chemicals for cosmetics. Be careful out there!*

The gathered members of the Cabal, especially those new to the story, gasped. Pleiadians who choose to incarnate in animal form had an extra vulnerability.

Sherman had arrived from the Pleiades into the suit of a puppy precisely to work with Caroline. They'd been kindred spirits for eons. He liked his "job" as the wise old dog. Little children flocked to pet him and squat down and look into his big, sad eyes. He didn't have to pretend to be a human scholar, or even a saint, or do menial human work to provide for his food and housing. Most of his life took place at the level of human's knees. As long as those knees were kind to him, he could do his work.

It even happens that some humans invade a new territory and think that the humans populating it already are savages, and that they need to be exterminated. People in America were known to bring shiploads of other humans from Africa and made them into slaves to serve the whims of rich people. They bred them like farm animals, sold them, raped them for pleasure, and mistreated them unto death.

Is there nothing stopping this abuse and torture? Asked the Calico.

We're here to raise their vibrations of the mean and witless. Many are comfortable in a life full of TVs, cars, fast food, and guns. But many of them suffer from mental problems, or just unhappiness. They might be unlucky, or indulge in pleasures that turn into addictions like smoking, alcohol, and opioids. They live believing that they are sinners and need to be punished. They control the freedom of women, giving them lives of indentured service to men, Sherman explained. *Just like some of them think that they will be 'saved' from a bad life by a religious faith, we think they will be 'saved' from a limited view of their place in the universe if they realize that meanness and greed are only bringing meanness back on them. If they realize that they are a piece of the Source that creates and works through love, they might change.*

Sherman told them about the mental hospital, that had been a warehouse for people deemed insane, or just useless. Patients were treated with electric shock and given lobotomies. Some of the treatments went were short-term and experimental, but the patient was damaged and diminished for the rest of his life. Of course, there were cures also, with patients calming down from being in a healing environment, growing strong, and leaving the hospital for integration back into normal society. But the diagnoses of mental disability and disturbance was a primitive art, and subject to experimentation and shallow understanding.

Sherman tried to temper the fear of Cabal members who worried about getting captured. It was alleged that there was a prison camp on Lopez Island in the San Juan Islands for 'suspected aliens and hybrids.' They would be subjects of research, but also torture and punishment for life. America used a near-permanent island prison for Muslim humans. It was not beyond imagining.

Secret government projects had locations, especially Area 51 in Nevada, for projects that included UFO investigations. It was euphemistically called Dreamland and Paradise Ranch. Any evidence of UFO presence was stored there, including reports of sightings from aircraft. A Top-Secret classification of all activities--black projects--prevented the public from learning anything about real evidence and conclusions about extra-terrestrial contact. Enough information had leaked, however, to give people interested in the science pause: any ET remains were at risk of being confiscated, dissected, and desecrated. Like Native American remains, they could become objects in a museum display case, or tossed in some dusty massive artifact storage facility. The view from mainstream society was that ET's don't exist. Their premise is: the idea of ETs is ridiculous. The idea is dangerous.

The Pleiades Cabal didn't know if they'd been identified and were being watched in Sedro Woolley. The underground press among aliens around the country spoke of being stalked by mysterious helicopters, marked "USA." There were many stories of humans who had had contact with UFO's and ET's, talked about it, and disappeared soon after.

Thus, were the varieties of sentient beings in human form, and maybe alien hybrids, who were in some fashion outside of mainstream society.

Even their own wilderness ally and neighbor, Trollop, was an example. He wasn't part of the Cabal, but a man who would understand the Cabal if he knew of it. (Or so the Cabal thought.) He himself "graduated" from Northern Hospital when it closed in 1973. Patients were released and given one-way bus tickets to destinations as far as San Francisco. They arrived in strange cities and towns with about $50 in their pockets, no address, and joined the street people. If they were lucky, they found a place to stay in homeless shelters. Trollop had already been wandering off the Hospital grounds for years and knew his way around the forests between Sedro Woolley and Mount Baker. Alleged a veteran of the Vietnam War, he was missing toes and fingers, and avoided conversation. Or, he might have been one of many mountaineers who had gone to Alaska to seek adventure and fortune, had some bad years through extremely harsh winters, and come south to Washington for the climate. Like a Yeti, he lurked in the woods and survived in the woods, willy-nilly, with his dog Jackson, a German short-haired pointer. The dog Jackson was in the Cabal, but his great duty was to be a companion and guardian to Trollop. Trollop was a fixture in their woodlands. They had in common a great wish to avoid the harassments of mainstream folk.

Many people will not agree with us, warned Sherman. *Sometimes their reaction is to be hostile. Sometimes their reaction is to push you out of their lives, or at least out of their view.*

They all knew that fear itself was an enemy: negative vibrations can cloud thinking and lead to poor decisions and mistakes. In an Earthly body, including mammal bodies, the hormones that trigger a fight-or-flight response are hard to suppress. But avoiding visibility in "normal" society was not the only agenda of those on the margins. The Cabal's mission was to raise the vibrations of the Earth. They had to survive in order to accomplish it. To survive and avoid the worst--exposure, mockery, maiming, torture, death--The Find, in a lunch box, in a tree, had to be kept out of the hands of Area 51 types.

No!

MUCH TO MOLLY'S SURPRISE, Esme and Simon were up early the next morning. She remembered that they'd been up late the night before, chasing bats. There was no rain last night, so it was an opportunity for the children to enjoy being out at night, navigating darkness.

"What's up, you two?" she asked. She knew about a club with interests in the galaxies, and superpowers, even the word "Pleiadian," but she herself was a total earthling, and happy. Her interest was the farmer's market, and the community around it.

"We saw something cool last night but it was too dark to investigate," explained Esme. "We want to go back and find it in the daylight. It might be something a fox will drag away. We couldn't tell what it was."

"Oh. A little science experiment?" It was Sunday morning, and a great chance for the kids to take their time wandering the woods, thought Molly. They were all heart-sore from Caroline's passing and needed slow time to calm the grief and distress of having their world change overnight. She needed some time to herself too.

"Yeah," said Simon, "We'll be back for lunch, okay?"

"Okay, kids, have fun." Molly felt good that they had something that drew their attention. She would have a quiet morning. Donald could sleep in.

They both took up small backpacks, stocked with an apple and a nut bar. Pip woke up and hurried through his dog food dish. The three left.

They got to the Cedar Hole about twenty minutes later. A morning dew glistened on leaves. The ground was damp, sending a fresh smell into the air. Fat slugs made their way through grasses, some directly on the barely-worn deer path, leaving a rope of slime marking their route. Every living thing was busy with the tasks of enjoying an earthly existence.

Esme knelt at the foot of the Cedar Hole so she could reach all the way up inside the hollow. First, she pulled out the branches they had stuffed as filler in the lower section. On first try, she reached as high as possible, but she could not feel the edges of the metal box. Her hand brushed the sides of the rough cavity over and over, each time a little more frantic.

"I don't remember pushing it up so far, Simon," she sighed. "We didn't have a lot of time yesterday."

She leaned down and reached up again. Nothing. Nothing.

"Simon, you try." She pulled her arm back to make room for him.

He lay on the ground next to the hollow and reached his skinnier, shorter arm, up inside. "Hand me a stick." A stick about a foot long went up the hollow beyond his hand. The cavity narrowed there to a point where a lunch box would never fit, even if you pounded it up.

"Wow. I don't know," he rolled away. He lay on his back, on the wet ground and grasses, his hand still resting in the opening. "Ugh."

"Ugh," said Esme.

Ugh, said Pip.

"Please, please be there. Simon, please try again," she said.

He rolled back toward the tree and pushed his arm up inside, holding the stick. "Nothing."

The three sat in a cluster, getting their bottoms wet and muddy. The early morning sunshine was no consolation. Esme started to cry.

"No, no." She sobbed. "Caroline will be so disappointed. How could this happen?"

We tried, said Pip. *Esme, no mistake. We did what we could.*

"I feel like we missed something. What could be going on here?"

"Let's ask Harold if he saw anything after we left," Simon said. "What if some other creature smelled us out here last night and came to investigate."

"And walked off with a metal lunch box?" Esme choked. "What are the chances?"

"I don't know. It's impossible!" said Simon. "It just can't be!"

I'll find Harold. See you at home, okay, you two? Pip got up and licked leaves from the back of his legs.

When they got home, Esme ran to her room to hide her flushed and tear-smudged face. She dove into her bedding and cried into a pillow.

Molly intercepted Simon. "How was your adventure?"

"Okay." He took his jacket off and hung it where it should go.

"What's with Esme?"

"I think she's sad about Caroline," said Simon. "She just got sad."

"Oh. My." Molly pulled him to her and hugged him. "You guys. We're all sad. Let me know if you want a sandwich or something. What a hard time for us."

"Thanks, Mom. I'll come down to get sandwiches, okay?"

"Sure." She watched him walk slowly up the stairs to their bedrooms. She knew that a sudden turn in mood was not unusual when people were processing grief. Her own feelings were turbulent, and she was trying to be a stable, nurturing presence, but she too felt like curling up with cocoa and having a good cry.

Harold had nothing to report. He'd made his foxy rounds in the night, after their stop at the Cedar Hole. True, he had taken off in another direction. His normal territory was three square miles. He had to maintain it by marking it with urine; some of the animals were quite familiar with his "scent stations." He could travel fast, up to forty-five miles an hour, and his sense of sight, hearing and smell were extraordinary. Even these special powers had yielded no sign that something was amiss at the Cedar Hole. That was unbelievable. Something was wrong.

Simon Flies

THE LAST THING SIMON SAW when he went to sleep at night was the ceiling of his room painted to display the night sky. Donald and Molly had picked up on his fascination with outer space and galaxies. After an intensive early mania for dinosaurs and the earth in the dinosaur era, and then easing into super-heros, including pajamas, capes, and helmets, Simon liked to speculate about what it was like to be on the moon, and the types of space ships that his entertainment universe offered him. Donald was a Trekkie fan and the two of them could watch Star Trek reruns and Star Wars movies over and over again. It was their signature pastime. Much of their conversation was the recalling and reliving favorite scenes and everything about them: the characters, the setting, dilemmas, plot twists, and technologies.

"What character would you want to be," asked Donald, "of all?" Donald himself had escaped the confusions of childhood through massive immersion in Star Trek. Sharing it with his son was a daily dose of familiarity between them. You could not separate their passion with this world from their bond for each other.

"Spock, of course," said Simon.

"Why?"

"He's smart. He's the science officer. He's half-Vulcan. He shows no fear." Simon had photos of Spock taped to his bedroom walls.

"And who would you want to be in Star Wars?"

"Chewbacca, hands down."

"What? He's an animal," Donald kidded.

"No, he's not. He's a Wookiee. They're also very smart, and, they're loyal to their honor family."

"And who's your honor family? How can you be a Wookiee without it?" Donald smiled. The two might not have sports that they shared, like baseball, but they were on the Star Trek team together.

"I'm not saying, Dad. They can also keep a secret," Simon said, taking a bite from his sandwich.

Donald leaned back trying to keep a straight face. He'd hoped for another answer. "Okay, Simon. Maybe you'll introduce me sometime." Now his smile was fake. The smile he thought a Dad should make, not the way he felt.

He knew preteen kids need to pull away from parents and start to shape their own identity, but he didn't welcome it. It would be nice to stay tight in a fantasy world with his son for a long time, and to be his closest ally and friend there. Stay special. Best buds. Other dads told him of watching their teenage sons disappear into their rooms right after dinner, increasingly seeking to be alone instead of playing in the living room, watching TV, jostling with Dad. Donald didn't have lots of free time, time to spend driving off into the woods and taking long hikes on weekends with his kids. He often had to work on Saturdays to cover for somebody else, and got good money for it. Then he had endless dad chores, too, keeping a house repaired and a yard decent.

Simon woke to sense a presence in his pitch-dark bedroom. There wasn't much ambient light but he knew from prior events that a dark shape stood there, waiting for him to wake up gently. Sometimes there was a soothing humming sound. (Pip could wake him with a soft grunt too, since his mind knew it well too.) He wasn't afraid. His visitors had become a familiar adventure that he welcomed. After maybe five years, the occasional visit of a dark shape had become a happy moment in his night, like an expected vision of a bright full moon or a surprise full-blown snow storm out his window. Natural, sweet, fascinating.

During early visits, the dark shape, whom he now called Glyph, at first was like an imaginary friend. He or she or it would show him how to levitate his toys, and make him laugh. Glyph might dance around the room like a flashing laser pointer. He (let's settle on this) was about four feet tall, skinny, with overly long arms and legs, three "fingers" and a thumb, like a fleshy bird's foot without the claws. Standing on two feet. His head was comically large, with large dark blue eyes that made him look more like an insect than a human. There was no mouth and small pointy ears on a bulbous head, with a thatch of light hair like a cartoon character. His skin was a bluish-gray, and rubbery, like a Dolphin's, only dry. Glyph "told" him things that Simon "heard" in his head. Simon didn't make any sounds back, when they talked, either. He'd learned to speak telepathically.

Glyph now took him by the hand and pulled him up out of bed. In the dark, they passed through the room, and then through the walls of the room, out into the back yard high over a tree--like Peter Pan, or the ET in the movie--and then they zipped instantaneously into a space ship. It was as if the two of them turned into energy bodies at will. In the space ship, it was like Disneyland: consoles and screens. Simon was shown areas of the Earth, and then fly-overs far into space, other galaxies. He was shown symbols that could have been maps, and a lab of mineral samples that he didn't recognize. He was taught to draw and write in the form of holograms, having beams of light extend from his hands. He watched a healing process practiced between ET's and was gradually taught to try it himself. It was like Reiki--hands passing over a body part--but the mental focus of energy was something he needed to learn and improve. This was to become Simon's secret super-power: the ability to heal, so they spent more time on that than on telepathy or clairvoyance, or getting to know the galaxies and the energy forms that populate them.

After Simon returned to his body back in his bed, the experience was like a faint memory. His visitors usually erased the details of the excursion and he recalled them only later when he was walking alone in the woods or sitting beside the river, thinking about things. Somehow, he knew they knew where he was and how he was, like guardian angels, but hands-off. All the extra learning was something he kept to himself. The heightened sixth sense he'd gained was the same as Esme's.

In the morning, Esme just knew he'd been away and said nothing. It's not like kids talked about how pretty the moon was last night, or how they watched the snow fall. She'd heard a little about Glyph and the wonders of the spaceship. She remembered that she'd had Lulu the sprite as her companion. The "trips" seemed like an extension of Simon's existence--his relationship to entities that came in the night. Like a special hobby. Another club. Caroline had explained that there were transfers of information, and powers, that were part of the Cabal's mission, especially related to healing souls. Like the characters in Star Wars, each member of the Cabal was different in his very composition and personal mission. Esme found herself glad for the sense of participating in Simon's "night life," like a hobby just between the two of them.

PART TWO: UGH

Chemistry Class

MOLLY WAS VACUUMING THE LIVING ROOM, mid-morning in early September, when the phone rang. She dashed to the phone docked in the kitchen. Donald had already left the house for his job at a bakery in Anacortes and the kids had gone back to school.

"May I speak to Mrs. Jensen? This is Charles Bright, the principal of Simon's school."

"That's me. Hello." Molly moved to perch on a kitchen stool. She'd met the man once at a parents' night at school.

"I hate to bother you, but we have a situation here."

"Okay." She put her other hand on the phone as if to steady it. She didn't have much of an impression of the man but knew he was respected among the parents.

"With Simon. He's okay, don't worry." He spoke in a steady tone, practiced in calling parents out of the blue, jarring their daily routines when they thought they were free of the kids for a minute.

"But." She leaned down and put her elbows on the kitchen counter-top.

"Well, his class had a chemistry segment today. They were exploring light. Different kinds of light. Light spectrum. That sort of thing."

"Okay. Sounds good." Molly never liked chemistry but was glad the school was good enough to teach science.

"When they turned on a pure ultraviolet light, a strange thing happened. Regarding Simon."

"I see."

"There were places on his body that glowed in that light. The looked like marks or tattoos. They glowed a bright blue-green."

"What?" Now she leaned back against the wall, trying to imagine. "What kind of marks?"

"In many places. Patches of light. Some triangles. The back of his head, on his temples, forehead. Earlobes. Wrists. That's just areas of skin that show."

It was still hard to imagine. "Is he all right?"

"Oh sure. He can see them too, of course. The whole class can see. They're pretty much shocked."

"And then what happened?"

"The teacher took him to the nurse's office. She couldn't find anything special on these places, under normal light. No breaks in skin. No bruises."

"Then he's okay." She landed a downbeat on the last word, stating it clearly, for confirmation.

"He's fine. But I think you need to take him to a doctor. The kids had a Geiger counter in the classroom. It didn't register any radioactivity. I know that's crazy, but that's what they thought of doing."

"Well, that was handy."

"He's in my office now. I don't know that this is an emergency, but maybe he could use a break from the attention. He needs to calm down. It's been quite a drama as you can imagine."

"I can imagine. I'll be right there." Molly hung up and rushed to get her purse and car keys.

At the principal's office, Simon was nonplussed. He was sitting in the reception area reading a book from his backpack.

"Oh Simon! Are you okay?" Molly ran to him.

"Yeah."

She held him by the shoulders and looked closely at his earlobes, his temple, and then his wrists. She could see nothing special. "What's going on?"

He shrugged. "I seem to be radio-active but not really. You can only see it with an ultraviolet light."

"Can you show me?" Molly looked to the principal.

"Sure, let's go to the science teacher's office. He's got a black light."

The three of them walked down the hall. Classes were in session so there were no other people in the hall.

In the teacher's office, they turned out the lights. The teacher turned on a portable, battery-powered black light that was sold as a detector for pet urine on carpets and such. It was simple: a six-inch fluorescent tube mounted on a handle with a battery in it.

Simon's body lit up. He was suddenly decorated with bright glowing blobs of light, in a rather beautiful shade of blue-green. He was decorated like a Christmas tree. Molly gasped. The principal had seen it earlier, so he was less surprised.

"Simon! What's going on?" She looked to the teacher.

"We don't know. The light of course causes fluorescence in certain materials, like blood, urine, and saliva." Over Simon's head, he mouthed "also semen" to the two adults. "The police use it in forensics, to find bodily fluids that you can't see."

"But that's not the answer, is it?" Molly looked at him, incredulous. "He's not been spotted with bodily fluids, don't you think? You think somebody painted him with gunk?"

"No, he's not." The teacher chuckled, then stopped himself. "He's not bleeding in all these places. And you can see tiny patterns within the blob of fluorescent area, like tattoos. But when we turn the light off, we can't see them, even the outline."

"And they're not radioactive, right?" said the principal.

"Right." The teacher chuckled again, and then stopped himself. "The kids immediately jumped on it. Behind my back. But that's not totally out of whack to try. Nothing to do with ultraviolet light, however. We'll be talking about that. Right, Simon?" He put an affectionate hand on Simon's shoulder.

"Yeah. That was sort of cool." He was still nonplussed.

"Hey Simon," said the teacher leaning toward him, "You know that insects, birds, and some mammals can see near-UV directly? They don't need the lamp."

Simon smiled. "Wow. That means they can see this, right?"

"Right," the teacher said.

The principal could tell that they were getting lost in the magic. "Mrs. Jensen. I think you should at the least take Simon home so things cool off. I don't know what kind of doctor would know about this, but I leave that to you."

"Right," said Molly. "I'll talk to my husband. Simon, get your backpack. Let's go." She picked up his jacket. She borrowed the black light device.

Simon seemed reluctant to be the subject of any kind of emergency, and mostly wanted to stay near the teacher and talk about what happened. He also wanted to ask his Cabal whether they could see the spots without the ultraviolet light.

A visit to a dermatologist a few days later revealed nothing. None of his medical instruments found any skin condition that could explain the effect of the light. The areas that looked like a tattoo were normal in regular lighting.

"Simon, what do you think is going on?" asked Donald, at home. They were all sitting in the living room, watching TV. "Where have you been that's putting these marks on your body?"

"I dunno," he said, looking at his hands. "It could be my night friends." He glanced at Esme.

Donald and Molly's eyes widened as they looked at each other. "What night friends?" Donald kept his voice even. He knew about Esme's imaginary friend. That wasn't new. This was.

"They come and we do things."

"What kind of things?" said Molly, breaking into a sweat.

"Go up to a space ship. Hang around." He looked as Esme again. She'd heard it before.

"Space ship?"

"Seems like."

"What do you mean 'seems like?'" asked Donald.

"We don't actually *go* there. They come to visit and then we find ourselves there."

"Just like that?" He was impressed with his son's imagination.

"Yeah. I don't remember a lot. I just wake up in my bed later. They're nice. And fun."

"Fun?" Molly looked at Donald.

"They show me neat stuff. Lasers. Places with lights."

"Do they do anything to you?"

"I don't know." He shrugged.

"Do they hurt you?"

59

"Oh no, Mom." Simon looked at his mother in disgust. "I said they're friends."

Donald leaned forward. "Does this happen very often?"

"Every few months."

"Can you tell me next time it happens?"

"Not really," said Simon. "It's a surprise, and totally quiet. I hardly know it's happening and then it's over. It's between me and them."

"Can you tell me *after* it happens again, then?" Donald tried to get Simon's full attention. An imaginary world was one thing, an obsession was something else.

"Sure. If I remember it."

"And ask them to stop it?" Donald's face seemed forced into a neutral expression.

"Oh, I don't know. I don't want them to stop."

"We don't like this," said Molly. "Can you imagine that we're afraid for you?"

"I know. But there's nothing bad going on," said Simon.

"Can you have them talk to us?"

"Okay. I'll try." Simon got up to go to bed. He didn't want his parents to make him do anything, at this point. He wasn't even sure they knew about telepathy, so how could they even have a talk? Who could explain vibrations, and dimensions, and energy bodies? He'd been to school, after all. It was complicated.

A week later, Esme was biking home after school when Carl-Crow swooped in front of her to get her attention. She stopped and straddled her bike in the middle of the dirt road. Carl landed on a tree.

It's Simon. We've got to get over to the Bug House grounds. Some boys have taken him there. Carl said.

"What? What did you see?" asked Esme, gripping her handle bars tighter.

They were pulling him. A bunch. He had a belt around him, pinning his arms.

"Was he crying?"

No, but he was telling them to stop. We've got to go! Carl pumped his wings.

"Go!" Esme jumped on her pedals. They were about a mile from the grounds. It would take Esme at least ten minutes.

Carl flew ahead to scout where they'd gone. He also swooped around calling anyone in the Cabal who was in "hearing" range.

Esme finally got to the long dirt road leading into the grounds. She pedaled as fast as she could, in a controlled panic. She saw Carl in the sky leading her to one of the old buildings. She'd been there before. The inside was a wreck, covered in graffiti. There was garbage all over the concrete, weeds. It smelled of urine and feces. The walls had red streaks meant to suggest gruesome activities but they could have been put there by teenagers intentionally playing zombie or acting out horror films. She parked her bike out of sight, and left her school bag with it.

In a creepy small concrete chamber, five boys had Simon up against a wall. Several held rocks in their hands.

"You're an alien!" one of them shouted at him. "We're going to kill you before you kill us!"

"No I'm not!" protested Simon, his eyes wild with adrenaline. "You don't know what an alien is!"

"Blue spots. That's creepy!"

"Who's your daddy?" shouted one. All the boys were slightly older than Simon. Probably not from his class but definitely from the neighborhood.

"You know who my dad is! Who do you think it is?"

"Aliens, that's who. You kidnap humans and experiment on them. You must be a plant!"

"Am not. You're crazy. Stop it! Just stop it! You're going to get into a lot of trouble!" Simon tried to fend them off. He wasn't crying, but clearly scared.

One of the boys went near Simon and kicked him. "I bet you're not even a human!"

Simon buckled. He was backed against a dirty gray wall covered with graffiti, peeling paint, and stains of food or feces that had been thrown against it. The place looked like a torture chamber that had been used before.

The others raised their rocks. Another boy went up to him and kicked him in the ribs as he knelt from the first hit. Then a rock hit him in the shoulder, and another on his cheek, cutting it open.

A stoning, thought Esme. Just like the creepy Taliban! They're going to kill him! She found her own large rock and stepped into sight. "You're going to have to do me too, you suckers!"

The boys turned to look at her. "What are you? The alien's girlfriend? Get out of here!"

Simon was as startled as they were. "Esme! Don't!"

"No way, suckers. I'm going to take you out before you touch my brother!"

Suddenly a rock came flying in her direction, missing her head by six inches. Then another hit the doorway just above her head.

"Esme, run! Please!" Simon shouted, now more anxious for Esme than himself.

Suddenly a gun went off, the bullet hitting the side wall next to the boys. Everybody ducked in terror. Then two hound dogs, howling like hunters that had just caught their prey, and a snarling German short-haired pointer bounded into the room and attacked the boys. The hound dogs were short but they could jump as far as the crotch of a boy, to give them a good scare. The pointer put fangs on one arm holding a rock, and then bit another.

The boys fell as they fought the dogs. As soon as they were free of a dog, they scrambled to their feet and raced to the entry where Esme stood. They pushed past her as she waved her big rock at their heads.

Finally, they were all gone.

The dogs sat down, panting.

Esme put her rock down and went to Simon. She unbuckled the belt around his arms.

"Simon," she choked. "Simon. Oh my god."

"I know," he said, kneading his arms where the belt had cut in. "Bloody awful." He turned to the dogs. "Thanks, Jackson, Sherman, Bailey. I owe you." He leaned against the wall and breathed hard. "And Esme." He sighed, pulling the bottom of his shirt up to his bleeding cheek.

She put her arm around him as they stumbled out of the chamber. She led him to her bike and got her book bag and bike. Sherman and Bailey walked them back to their house. Jackson disappeared into the woods, as they expected he would.

A Fix

THE DOCTORS IN THE EMERGENCY ROOM found lots of bruises and just two lacerations. Simon's cheek got three stitches.

Officer Kameron came to the hospital to talk to Donald while Simon was being treated.

Esme sat beside Donald, pale and quiet.

"Boys, huh?" Kameron said, taking out his pad. He was sweating from the exertion of having to move faster than usual.

Donald was incensed. Sedro Woolley could be a rough place with so many down-and-out families. There was a lot of domestic violence. A lot of anger. He hadn't been a recipient, even though as a black man he was a candidate for gratuitous slurs and aggressions. Being married to a white woman added to his candidacy for disapproval and resentment, harassment for violating the "laws of nature" according to certain folk. His family had moved away from the streets of Chicago to the Portland area to get away from the legacies of slavery, bad everything for blacks. He'd hoped to go to a "wild west" where there were few blacks and nobody knew to kick them around yet. A place where, he thought, you mixed in Chinese immigrants, Hispanics, Native Americans, and it was far from an urban ghetto. Here they were, in the wilds of Sedro Woolley, and his son was subject to gang violence. Rocks instead of guns, though. Not even knives, yet. It was just a matter of time.

"You're going to arrest them, aren't you? Those boys could have killed my son!" Donald stood up to face him.

"Now, now. Let's get all the facts first. You and I know there's a lot of fighting around here. The kids will go at each other sometimes." Kameron had indeed been to training on how to handle hysterical situations. Kids growing up in violent homes tended to be violent. They had to be tamed early and often, and sometimes they were just making their first mistake. Simon wasn't one of them, but he was a likely target.

"This is no 'going at it.' These boys took my son to the Bug House to kill him." Donald put his hands on his hips and started to shift from one foot to the other.

"I don't know, Sir. You have to tell me what happened, first." Kameron calmly pulled up his notebook and pen.

Donald stepped back and waved to Esme. "Tell him, please."

She gave him the overview, including the rocks hitting Simon, rocks aimed at her. She mentioned the gunshot. She looked back at her dad for approval. She'd rarely seen him so tense and didn't know what to do.

"Gunshot? Where'd that come from?" Kameron asked.

"Guns," said Donald. "Now we're getting familiar."

"I don't know," she said. "Out of nowhere. And only one. That's it."

"Nobody showed up with a gun?"

"No sir, Mr. Kameron," Esme remembered he told the kids to be polite when they talked to police. She gave him the names of the boys. Everybody knew everybody in Sedro Woolley. She could tell you where each of them lived.

"Well, sir," Kameron said to Donald, "I'll follow up and let you know. I'm sure sorry this happened. Must be quite a scare for you."

Donald had calmed down. The Officer's respectful tone was what he wanted to hear. He didn't want to hear denial. It wasn't "boys being boys" when they were out to stone a kid to death. This couldn't be happening in Sedro Woolley. He had to trust that, and it was hard. They already had to be careful about what people thought in Sedro Woolley--in spite of its great mix of eccentrics, ne'r-do-wells, fly-by-nights, former and current crazies, mavericks, losers, addicts, rich-bitches, and yes, normals. "Muggles." He thought their family had a shot at normal in a place like this. He didn't want his life to be ruled by sublimated racism every day, every single day. He would even grow his hair long if that would make him a normal, as in aging hippy or hard-working farmer. He'd been ecstatic to find a place in a large, innovative bread-making business. It was an escape from traditional occupations and their traditional biases against blacks.

The next morning was Saturday, so the family slept in. There would be no chores sending anybody out the door early. Molly made pancakes and bacon, making the whole house smell good.

Three of them were sitting at the breakfast table when Simon came down. The sun was shining, for a change. Pip was sun bathing on the rug, spread-eagled and conked, as if drunk on pleasure.

"Oh, my baby," said Molly, who got up to give him a hug. "You must be sore all over. Sit down and have some bacon." She pulled a chair away from the small, round oak table.

Simon sat down, smiling at Esme. Then he smiled at his dad. "Thanks for taking care of me, Dad," he said. "Sorry to be a bother."

"You're not a bother to me, Simon," said Donald. "You're my precious son. We'll do everything we can to protect you." He reached a hand to touch Simon's arm.

"Yeah," said Esme. "Chill. Eat bacon." She was grinning at a plate full of pancakes smothered in syrup.

"Wait," said Molly, reaching over to his bad cheek. "What's this? There's three stitches, and healed skin. How could you heal so fast?" She looked over at Donald. The stitches would get absorbed eventually but the flesh had already closed into a smooth, fresh and soft surface. The sweet cheek of a ten-year-old.

"I don't know," Simon said, reaching for the plate of bacon. In front of him, a whole pound of strips was stacked on a Mexican-painted plate, bright and beautiful.

"Donald, it's healed up!" Molly said. She pushed her chair back and stood up, leaning on the table, toward Simon. "Look."

Donald reached over to turn Simon's face toward him. "Golly. Yes. I'll be darned. Strange. Simon?"

Simon put bacon in his mouth and reached for the pancakes. There were sounds of gleeful crunching.

Donald insisted that Molly take Simon to a psychologist to check out the "night visitors" thing.

"What do these visitors look like, Simon," the psychologist asked.

Molly and Simon were sitting on a sofa in his therapy office, designed to be cozy. There were paintings of sail boats on the walls. They were in Bellingham, a port on the Puget Sound, and home to many people who were into fishing, sailing, ferries, and kayaks. Sedro Woolley was too small to support a psychologist, but Bellingham was a ferry stop, the home of a university, and a growing community of people who were moving north in Washington state to get away from urban congestion. Even it if was just for weekends.

"Lights, mainly," said Simon. He wasn't eager to bring another person in on his secrets.

"Do they talk to you?" the man asked. He was in his forties, wearing a casual sweater, with bushy, graying hair. He too was in Bellingham for a slower pace.

"Sure. But mentally."

The man paused, not sure what that meant. "And what do they say?"

Simon shrugged. "Hello. We're here."

"Anything else?"

"How are you?" Simon smiled.

"Okay. They're nice, I get it." The psychologist shifted his position.

"Yes. Nice." Simon nodded.

"What do they do that you're finding fun?"

"They show me stuff."

"Like what?"

"A picture of galaxies." Simon folded his arms.

"Galaxies?"

"Yes."

"Anything else?" The psychologist had his pen ready.

"They teach me to talk mentally."

"Really?"

"Yes."

"And you can do that?"

"Sometimes."

"Can you make them come when you want?"

"I can call them. But I don't much."

"Why would you call them?"

"If I'm in trouble, I guess. I've never done it."

"Did you call them when the bullies took you to the Bug House?"

"No."

"Why?"

"I felt they would come if they had to." Simon sounded sure of himself, for once.

"But they didn't."

"No. Esme came. And Sherman. Bailey."

"Those are dogs?" He looked over at Molly, who nodded.

"Yes."

"How did they know you were in trouble?"

"They knew."

"I see." He'd tried to poke holes in the stories.

After more dialog like this the psychologist excused Simon and talked to his mother.

At home that evening, Donald grilled Molly. Esme knew this was going to happen, so she slipped down the stairs in her socks and sat on the bottom step, out of their sight. She pretended to be checking out her toes.

"He says that hearing voices is a symptom of schizophrenia. Or paranoia." Molly said.

"Schizophrenia? Really?"

"Really. Where a person talks to a hallucination. Schizophrenia doesn't usually arrive that early, in a child, but it can happen."

"And what do we do about it?" Donald was sitting on the couch next to Molly for this debriefing.

"There are medications. They keep the hallucinations down. People can live a normal life if they take medication," explained Molly.

"He recommended medication?" asked Donald.

"No, he can't prescribe. We have to go to a psychiatrist."

"A psychiatrist? More money?" It was a long way from a commune in Oregon, a simple life. There, in their shared young life, however, no hospitals, no police. Also, no children.

"Yes, Donald, if we think we want to medicate him."

"What do you mean, 'if we want to medicate him?'" Donald pulled away from her. "Pills? The rest of his life?"

"Yes. I think so. Or at least until the effect of the pills wear off, and then he'll need new pills."

"Molly, seriously?" He pulled away.

"Seriously. But I don't want any pills for my Simon." Molly crossed her arms.

"What?"

"He's not crazy. He's normal. He's not like the people in the Bug House. He's not like the homeless talking to themselves. He's thriving in school. He's smart. He's funny. Maybe he has a great imagination. I don't see any crazy there. Didn't you hear all the stories about the Bug House? People were put away because they were just a bit different? Or just difficult? Or they had no other place to go?"

"What about the Night people, Molly. Night people. What do you think that is?" No one talked about mental illness. His family had their hands full with hostility in public, anger, the many insults. Never troubles that all took place in your head.

71

"I don't know. But I won't give him pills for that!" Molly sat up straighter.

"But what if he does start talking to himself, or to some hallucination. What if he falls off the edge?"

"Let's wait for that, then. He's not acting crazy in school or at home."

"What about the blue glow on his body?"

"That's not his brain, Donald. Please don't lump all this together." She put her hand on his arm.

Donald brushed it off and stood up. "I do not want a crazy kid, Molly. I'll lose my job. What those boys did was like a lynching. We can't risk that. I do not want to see my son hanging from a tree with his balls cut off!"

"Donald. Stop." Molly stood up. "Those were school bullies. They were triggered by blue light. It's fear. We can watch for the crazy. The crazy is not happening. Simon is a sensitive, funny, smart, wonderful boy right now. Please don't spoil that." She put her hands on his shoulders for emphasis.

"I can't. I can't imagine my boy done in. I want to save him. I want him alive, and with me." He was crying. His tall frame bent forward, face in his hands.

"I know. I want a live boy too. I want a happy, loving boy. Simon is that, and we're going to keep him that way. Sedro Woolley is not Hell." She pulled his head to her shoulder. "We'll stay close to our boy. Those bullies will be punished. One day at a time, Donald. One day."

Esme grabbed her toes and squeezed through the long silence that followed.

Consultation

"Mom," CALLED ESME AFTER BREAKFAST, "We're going out to the woods for the rest of the day." It was an overcast Sunday in September, nothing special.

"Okay," Molly called back from the kitchen. "Don't do anything I wouldn't do." She laughed, and heard Esme laugh back. It was a family joke. Esme knew that her parents had been hippies in Oregon, and "normal" and "safe" was not their life style.

Pip, did you tell everybody to head out? Esme transmitted to Pip, who was waiting by the door.

Sure did, he answered, his little butt bouncing down the back stairs as he followed Simon out the back door.

They walked through the fields and patches of forest about a mile towards the Bug House grounds.

There were dog trainers who used the entrance to the parking lot as a miniature training course. They came with a truck that pulled a large trailer full of props, which were set up in the ample space. In a second covered truck were a few crates big enough to hold German Shepherd dogs. The trainers set up a tent and folding camp chairs under it, in case of rain. Their customers would drive in, park their cars, and bring a dog over for training exercises, which included running through an obstacle course.

The regular German Shepherd dogs knew the Cabal. Somehow, they too were in on telepathy. From a different planet?

The animals enjoyed seeing each other from a distance. The trainers were apprehensive seeing the dogs Pip, Sherman, and Bailey off leash. They were afraid of surprise attacks from either side. They knew that their big dogs could chew through most other dogs. The problem was vet bills, and possible law suits. There were no signs in the park that forbade people from having dogs off leash. It wasn't that kind of place. People in the country didn't like to be told what to do. They didn't like to be treated like a crazy person in a city park. Also, these people had trained their dogs pretty much, so bug off.

Hey, Guardians of the Galaxy, joked Sherman when he saw the German Shepherds. *We worship you!* He was being ironic.

You may pass, said their lead dog, also ironically. He was fond of Sherman the hound dog. He paused from making a little Chihuahua walk through an obstacle course.

The Chihuahua also spoke up: *Yo! Come here and set me free!* They all laughed.

The Cabal passed through the parking lot, taking a trail through the brush toward the shell of a building that had been a school for children of the staff at Northern Hospital. They'd discovered the school some time ago, playing nearby.

Children of the staff at Northern Hospital had been treated well when it was in operation. Their parents had been doctors and nurses at the hospital. The hospital cafeteria sent over food for them. It was easy to feed the children along with up to 1,500 patients and the full staff, at its peak population. However, the children were isolated from the town. Mainly, they had each other as playmates. They were close-knit in their isolation, even though some were recent immigrants.

One day, there was a big fire in the school in which a large group of children perished all together. It started when the pipe going up from a wood stove broke from the wall, releasing heat and flames up the wooden wall behind the stove. Now, the spirit children stayed close to each other and close to the school grounds, the scene of their death.

When the Cabal got to the old school building, it was covered in fog, even though it was set on a slight hill.

"Hey, hey," Esme called as if coaxing cows in from a field. "If you're home, please come out. We need your help." She knew ghosts could get pretty bored, in an abandoned deteriorating building, for lack of stimulation.

"Come and see us!" whispered Simon, picking up from Esme. "Please."

The Cabal stood at the foot of the hill. The dogs sat on haunches. Carl-Crow was tracking with them through the treetops. The cats had opted to stay back home and have a snooze indoors, as usual.

Almost imperceptibly, the fog shifted into clusters on the banks of grass leading up to the school ruins. The Cabal looked at each other, silent, implicitly signally, *Don't say anything. Wait.*

Then, like a photo being developed in a darkroom, the image of children came through. Some were clearer than others. They were standing in front of the school as if they had been called out to pose for a photo. There were little ones, and big ones. Clearly, they were used to being a group, because their attention was outward, toward the Cabal.

Some sounds came through. They were the sounds of children you might hear if you were standing outside a school, near a window. Indistinct sounds, mixing laughter and high-pitched voices exclaiming amongst themselves, at various pitches and volumes: "Mine! Over there! Let go! Ha ha! Gotcha!"

"Is Ben here?" Esme asked. Ben was older, maybe her age. She had thought about the fact that he would never age, and she would. He was her favorite, and less child-like that the little ones. He could interact beyond one word.

A taller figure toward the left of the group shimmered enough to stand out.

"Ben," said Esme slowly, "we lost a lunch box. Lunch box. Have you seen it?"

They waited possibly ten minutes while the images of individuals faded and came back, with the fog getting in the way at the wrong time.

Finally, they heard Ben's typical laugh. "Ha ha."

"Lunch box," said Esme. "Can you point?"

They waited again. It was getting chilly just standing there. The wet grass made it unpleasant for dogs to sit.

The shape of Ben took a step in their direction, and stopped. He slowly swiveled his head back and forth.

"No," said Esme, interpreting. "No." She looked at her friends. They seemed to concur with her take on the message.

"Thanks, Ben. You take care now." She waved a friendly hand to him, smiling, and wondering where he went when he disappeared from their sight.

"Well," she said turning to the Cabal, "Let's go check Samuel and Tabitha." They turned away from the shimmering images of children, and took a path into the brush.

This response from Ben was most discouraging. Ghosts, like foxes, could cover quite a bit of territory, at least in sensory terms. They had a radar for living people, and in this kind of isolated place, they would be entertained to watch the living. They would find it fun to see somebody around, regardless of what they were doing.

The Cabal headed over to the former laundry, which had been maintained by a young couple, Samuel and Tabitha. The old laundry held the remains of massive pipes and plumbing that once channeled water into large washing bins. A hospital with a thousand people had a lot of bedding and towels to keep clean. Patients helped with the labor, but the facility took experience. The couple received free housing in exchange for managing the small building. They adored each other and adored their little piece of turf, putting up flower boxes on the few windows of what was a little sweatshop.

The Cabal had to pull away vines and overgrown bushes to get to the door. There were signs over the doorway asking visitors to stay out of the buildings for safety reasons: rotting wood was falling from the roof and rafters.

The Cabal knew that one corner was favored by the ghostly pair as it was closest to their daytime stations in the past. It was steamy, cold and dark. The couple was part of the migration of tar heels from North Carolina. They died when a boiler near the room where they slept exploded in the night. It was quick. At least they were together.

"Samuel," said Esme, addressing the corner. "Tabitha."

"We need a favor," said Simon, learning to take part in the conversation.

"Lunch box. Missing," said Esme. "Help."

They could hear an occasional sound as if someone had just said something in a quiet train that passed through quickly. The sound came in quietly, swelled, and then faded.

"Please, please. Samuel," said Esme again.

The Cabal was huddled in a doorway facing the corner.

"Lunch box," said Simon.

They waited, again. A mist built up in the corner. Samuel's face came through on the upper wall, hovering. After a while, Tabitha came through also, as if seated below.

There was

no sound for a long time.

Then, there was a whoosh as if an invisible train was passing and then a faint word: "Okaaaay."

"Okay?" Esme repeated. "You mean it's okay? Is that what you mean?

"Okaaay," faintly.

"But where?" asked Esme, frustrated but pacing her words.

Samuel's face flickered and faded as if it were running on a failing battery. Tabitha simply vanished. They were clearly done messaging.

"Help," pleaded Simon. "Help."

The image went blank. All they could see was the weather-beaten concrete wall.

"Oh, man," said Esme. "That was almost just a 'hello.' Darn it!" She tried to keep her voice down, not to insult the ghosts, who were long-time acquaintances by now. She put her hands over her mouth in a mock scream of frustration. Then she remembered ghosts were watching even when you couldn't see them. "Okay. Samuel, Tabitha. Okay. We think. Thanks." She wanted to be polite. They were friends, after all.

The group picked their way through vines with thorns that had taken over narrow pathways leading away from the building. There wasn't enough traffic in this part of the grounds to trample the plants and clear them away.

"Ugh," said Esme, almost to herself. "No help at all. But Samuel knew something. He just wasn't going to tell."

I know, said Pip. *Ghosts are not reliable. I've always thought so.*

They're not really guardians, you know, said Sherman.

"No? What are they, then?" asked Simon.

Lost, mostly. They're waiting for something to happen. They're stuck in a dimension, like glued in. Ghosts are people who suffered a great trauma at death, and they are staying near the site of the trauma while they try to grasp what happened to them.

"Do they ever go anywhere?"

Somebody has to help them heal. They need to understand what happened and recover their awareness of the reality of the incident. Their brains are suspended in dissociation. They need help. Help from people in this life or from other ghosts, said Sherman.

"But he did say 'okay,' didn't he?" asked Esme. "Whatever that means."

He did.

"Why can't they just help?" Simon said. "It's just selfish. What good is having ghosts all over if they don't watch the place?"

Busy, Sherman said. *Kind of stuck on their death. Don't really mean to be mean.*

Esme had a horrible feeling. Caroline wanted them to do the job, she thought. What if they couldn't?

The spoken words of ghosts--according to ghost whisperers--hinted at trauma and abuse. Esme once asked Caroline if a ghost could be healed of its complaints. She said, "Of course. But ghosts don't manifest long enough to engage a healer. They just throw out their wails and cries and then hide. It's clever avoidance. And harmless to the rest of us. There's enough misery among the living humans that we're not going to spend a lot of time on ghost rescue and ghost therapy."

She said that those talking to unhappy ghosts advised them to "get over it" and "move on" but the ghosts were stubborn. As if they could not stop. It was like an addiction. Everybody knows you can't make somebody quit an addiction unless they want to. You can just beat them over the head with your advice, without effect, over and over.

That's why there were no portals on the hospital grounds. Over-populated with crazy.

Simon and His Friends

ONE SATURDAY MORNING Simon didn't come down for breakfast. It was past the time the two usually slept in. Molly had gone to her job at the farmer's market. Esme finished her cereal, put the dishes in the sink, and went upstairs to check on him.

He was lying in bed, looking at the galaxy on his ceiling. He looked tired and pale, but content.

"Simon. What's up?" she asked. The room was dark, the drapes drawn. The ceiling used reflectors so it was like a starry sky scape. "What are you looking at?"

"My blue energy body. I can see where blocks are, and some are making me sick. But don't worry, in a few days I can clear them."

"Did you get sick? Did they make you sick?"

"I'm good. Took a trip."

"You did? Can you tell me? Do you remember?" She sat down on his bed, like Molly would, if he had the flu or something. Usually the two of them spoke lying down spread around the room.

"I remember a lot. I was just remembering. It's a lot." He sighed.

"Do you hurt?"

"No, no. Although they did stick a long needle up my nose and into my brain."

"What?" She resisted the urge to touch his nose.

"It went 'pop' way up in my brain. I think they implanted a little thing. Somehow, I know that. 'Cause I think they took one out before."

"Did it hurt?"

"It hurt a little. But Glyph just puts his hand on my brow, and then I don't feel the pain. It was quick. Like something you'd do in a doctor's office. Routine."

"What's that thing doing to you?"

"It's growing my vibrations. My healing energies. Also, they can use it as a tracker. But somehow, they don't need a tracker to find me. Also, they can receive information from it. Check on me."

"And that made you tired?"

"Oh no. It was the trip to the Pleiades that made me tired. Many light-years, Glyph said."

"How did you travel?"

"You know they just float me out of my body, right? Well on the ship, they put me into a glass case, filled it with fluid, so I could withstand the travel process. Glyph says it was 500 light years away. Maybe it stressed me. Maybe for sure it stressed me."

"Pleiades? I'm jealous." Esme knew she wasn't 'chosen' for direct contact, but she was allowed to know everything Simon could remember. "What did you see?"

"First we stopped on a really gray planet. No green stuff, just rocks. There were creatures there like ugly frogs with eyeballs sticking out. Esme, I wish you could have seen that!"

"But that wasn't the Pleiades?"

"No. Then we went further." Simon turned on his side. He was waking up.

"They asked me what we eat. I tried to explain spinach, and squash. They barely know 'green' and 'yellow.' They can't imagine chewing stuff."

"What do they eat?"

"They tried to explain it. It's like a smoothie. I did NOT want to try it. It might kill me. Although, Glyph gave me a squirt of something when I needed to be relaxed. When I got really nervous."

"Did you see any aliens besides Glyph? Does he come for you alone?"

"No, no. He comes with a party. Maybe a party of five. They are shorter than him, and wear dark blue coveralls. About four and half feet tall, gray skin, big fluid black eyes. They stand in a row and wait for him to talk to me."

"Are they scary?"

"No, no. They're like bees. They seem to act like a hive--they move together. Nobody talks. I told you that before. They 'think' together. They make me think of kobolds."

"Kobolds? The creatures in Dungeons and Dragons? Who are busy making traps and ambushing you? And they live underground?"

"Well I think they act more like watch-dogs here. They're like a little army of robots. But they seem to be alive, not machines. They're MUCH plainer than kobolds." He laughed. Kobolds looked like little dragons, with weapons.

"What was it like on the Pleiades?"

"Full of light beings. No 'things' except for a gigantic cluster of crystals. A fantastic feeling of love. It felt like Caroline was there for a minute. They were showing me what it's like when we're pure energy. It's like everybody is a rainbow."

"No bad guys?"

"Well, Glyph tells me there are bad aliens. You can tell, because they pressure you to do things. Bad things. They're devious. They're like toxic people. Their energy doesn't come from The Source. They take energy away from you. You have to block them."

"Block?"

"Surround yourself in light. A cloak of beautiful color. Bring to mind something that gives you a feeling of safety. Some pagans had 'spirit animals.' You might think of your Lulu. Put up a wall of mirrors that reflect outward. So whatever they send to you is bounced back at them and can't get through to you."

"Have you run into any?"

"No. Not yet. But they're around, he says. They scare people. You don't have a good feeling with them. They're like demons."

"Are you glad they're visiting you?"

Simon sat up. "Oh gosh, for sure! They're teaching me so much! I can see things other people can't see. I know things. They're teaching me to heal. We need healers. It's been true for humans through all of our time. You know, shamans. Getting visited by 'sky beings' and seeing 'chariots in the sky.' That was the aliens teaching man how to use powers we already have."

"But you don't already have those powers, you said. They're giving you powers."

"They're training me. They are 'waking' me. You have them too, but you need practice. A kind of concentration. I'll show you, next time I try to use them here."

"But what do they want? Why are they doing this for you?"

"They want us to wake up. They think the human race could destroy itself with poisons, bombs, fighting. They recruit us--the whole Cabal--to encourage an evolution to a more spiritually advanced species that is more positive. A new kind of human that will eventually inhabit earth after a long period of transition. We're part of the new population that resists the bad stuff, like violence and destruction. Atomic bombs that kill everything including all other species. They want us to see the Earth as part of a greater world that is really spirit. Part of The Source."

"Want some cereal?" Esme flung herself across the end of the bed, tired from trying to grasp what he said, which did not sound like a ten-year-old. Their secret was growing bigger.

Heretic

Roslyn Millhouse made a trip to the Sedro Woolley library every week looking for her next week's reading binge. The librarian Jane enjoyed watching out for her interests, and would set aside some new tome that might raise a smile in Roslyn. She read voraciously genres aimed at women, especially "clean romance." She loved the book covers, which she found stimulating, and then the long, fast read through many encounters between a woman like herself and a very attractive rich man: lots of moments of temptation, leading to a climax of getting engaged and most important, the wedding night whose details fell off the page. This was totally consistent with her also extremely religious bent, because she believed that Jesus wanted people to be pure, and sexual purity meant that they must marry and have children. Nowhere did Jesus say that a woman like Roslyn should not take the long road through fictional courtships, for example, stopping for fantasy picnics by the river, having long talks at the coffee shop, sipping one glass of wine on the front porch, or sharing fresh biscuits at your kitchen table, all colored by the heady smell of a dreamy man and hot blood coursing through your body. Not bad for a lady around sixty years old.

"You should check the book sale cubby," said Jane to Roslyn when she came into the library. "We just got a basket of books from that woman Caroline's house."

"Oh, thank *you*," said Roslyn, already trying to picture what flavor of fun Caroline's private reading life might offer to her.

Someone had taken a largish light-wooden fruit basket with wire handles and filled it with books. It stood out among the old cardboard boxes full of dusty, faded hard-bound books and cheap worn paperbacks. Motel managers often stopped by to pick up filler for a book shelf by their check-in desk. The books were all 25 cents each, just to give the impression that the reader was helping the library by making a sale. You could go to the nearest flea market and pay a few dollars for a whole box, but the presence of these books in the library gave them a certain cache, as if they were too special or too good to be sitting out in the sun next to stinky old shoes.

On the very top, the word "Jesus" caught her eye. When she picked it up and brought it into proper focus for her aging eyes, it was an experience she would retell many times, for the title was "The Laughing Jesus: Religious Lies." The "lies" part of the title was worrisome, but maybe the "Jesus is laughing" part was going to take her to a view of Jesus that was just a bit more fun than the gentle, loving Jesus of Sunday school tales. Like, maybe he is portrayed as a person who told jokes, or, he pulled pranks on the apostles, or, he delighted in the antics of baby animals and small children. Laughing. Like Santa Claus. Ho ho

Under that book were a couple of paperbacks with the name "Pleiades" in the title. Roslyn didn't know that word, but it sounded like a flower to her, rhyming with "peonies." Maybe Caroline had discovered an esoteric gardening hobby; she'd discovered a flower that Roslyn didn't know, and Roslyn could try it out, like a new flavor of coffee, or a brand of yogurt, or a kind of cake from the South. Maybe it was about cooking, and part of a series of cook books on a specialty like a kind of pasta, or an English pudding, or a cheese casserole that was particularly hard to make and people collected recipes and kept trying to make it. Like lasagna. She took up four books, along with the Jesus book. She didn't like to stand on her feet very long. There were no chairs in the book sale cubby, to discourage readers from settling in to read, blocking other people who came in to browse the treasures.

Well, she choked on her coffee the next morning. "The Jesus story is a Pagan myth." "His is a story that was made up by disciples who wanted to use his image for power." "The Bible is not true." "Jesus was elevated to the Son of God only in the 12th Century." "Garden of Eden, the virgin birth, Moses, Noah's Ark, the Exodus from Egypt. All fairy tales, to seduce believers into becoming followers."

Roslyn jumped to her writing pad:

"BLASPHEMY!

I am shocked to find books in the library's resale bin that are POISON to our young!!! There are Godless people among us. Heretics.

We must be vigilant in stamping out these lies! Some books supposedly from the house of Caroline Milarep (God rest her soul) were sitting out in broad daylight. We cannot HOPE to guide our YOUNGSTERS along the path of righteousness if they are exposed to such blasphemy. I ask the library to be more careful in 'recycling' people's libraries."

[signed] Roslyn Millhouse

Raymond Sharpshrifter got her letter the next day. He was the founder, editor, and delivery-person of the *Sedro Sentinel: the Real Deal*, an opinion-laden blatt that sold for $1 in grocery stores between the free real estate booklets and the gossip rags. He thought the secret to the sustainability of his tiny, local newspaper was to raise everybody's blood pressure and force them to sit down and write spitting opinions. Keep them awash in provocation.

That's how Molly came to see the letter--at the grocery store. She also saw the comments that were sent in response, and, of course, published.

Esme listened to a different side of her mother: angry, mocking the statements people were making:

"A teachable moment. We are inundated with garbage in supposedly respectable books."

"Fake news. Lies."

"Libraries should not censor. But there are limits to free speech."

"Just what kind of 'services' was she offering? And making a living at it!"

"Praise the Lord, our Father in Heaven. And his Son, Jesus."

"Blasphemy is sin. It should be a crime."

"People, just explain to me virgin birth, and a man rising after he died. If you reject science, you are indeed talking about myths and fairy tales."

"Mom," said Esme, "What's a virgin birth go to do with it? What does that mean?" Many of the comments made no sense to her. Her beloved Caroline was being turned into some kind of adult storm, and nonsense.

"Never mind, dear," Molly answered.

People who knew that Molly was a close friend of Caroline's were greatly embarrassed for her. When they saw her in public, they disappeared one way or another, not sure whose side to take. Many of Caroline's customers were under cover--they did not run around telling people that they had consulted a psychic. They simply put a sympathetic hand on Molly's arm and then walked away. An occasional check-out clerk did not make eye contact. Mud-slinging at a familiar member of their small community who had just died was unseemly, awkward. Even un-Christian. Did I mention: Caroline had made it hard for busy-bodies to label her dangerous. Now they had a handle.

Soon, vandals painted every other vertical board on the gate in front of her house black, to appear as if it was missing teeth. Raymond the journalist made sure to publish a photo, albeit on page three.

Esme and Simon dreaded the start of school next month.

There was no follow-up picture of those black boards, after they were painted over with colorful, cheerful flowers, by somebody, in the middle of the night.

"Mom," said Esme. "Some religious people are not very nice, are they?"

"They feel strongly that they have the only truth."

"What is the truth?"

Molly laughed. "We can't prove a lot of things." She did not want to explain a virgin birth, today. "People have working hypotheses. That's why it's called 'belief.'"

"What do you believe?"

"I believe that people are good, but we're imperfect. We have emotions and impulses that make us hurt ourselves and other people, sometimes without meaning to. What we want may blind us to what we can have, and we take it anyway. We have to have good manners, which is really respect for other people, and some rules about not hurting people. No murder, no killing. It gets very complex."

"How do you explain the way Caroline died?"

"I don't. It's a mystery to me. How do you explain it?"

"She disappeared, but she's not gone. We just can't see her."

"Oh my, Esme. You are getting to be quite the smart cookie!"

Esme smiled and went to the cabinet and made a grand gesture of taking an oatmeal-raisin cookie from a box there, smiled at her mom, and went upstairs. It wasn't funny. It was confusing. Scary.

Later that night, Molly took a stiff drink to sip in bed. Whiskey and vermouth were called for, not meditation. She leaned back on her pillows, sipping and sighing. Donald was reading a light mystery in one hand, and reached out with the other, to touch her arm in sympathy.

"They have a lot of nerve," muttered Molly. "Christians have committed genocide for centuries. They've had crusades against Jews, Protestants, Muslims, Native Americans. Witches. All in the name of God."

"It's not just Christians, Molly, it's fundamentalists, I think," Donald said gently. "The Romans were just as bad killing Christians because they weren't pagans."

"In the name of God. Terrorists. Assassins. Murdering their own for not being pure enough. Gandhi. Martin Luther King.

Malcolm X. Yitzhak Rabin." She sipped, as Donald tried to read another paragraph in his novel.

"I wish they would all Rapture themselves away. Leave us behind. Leave us alone. Go ahead. Make my day."

"There are some nice people you would miss, Molly," Donald said not taking his eyes from his book.

"I miss Caroline." She sobbed into her hand, taken by surprise. "Why did she have to go? She was only fifty, Donald. Why? I know she warned me. I just can't imagine living without her. My anchor. My heart. She said it was her time, and I just couldn't stand to hear it."

"I don't know, Molly. We all have some kind of clock. Or fate."

"Donald, what do you think really happened to Caroline?"

"I don't know, Molly. I don't know. Something like the virgin birth, we've got here. A miracle. A mystery."

"You know she learned some yogi tricks in India."

"I know. Ask Esme to research it in the library."

"Oh sure. That'll get around. Esme's trying to figure out Hindu ways of dying."

"Not all Hindus. Yogis." Donald tried to temper her mood.

"Well then Roslyn Millhouse is right. We are Godless."

The two of them had prided themselves on being unconventional. They were former commune members who wanted to escape society and pressures to conform. They knew there was a price to pay for being different--for being different and sometimes flaunting it. Now, in Sedro Woolley, you couldn't tell their lifestyle from the neighbors, until you had a deep conversation. However, there was a big difference, a difference that people cared about, that they couldn't hide: skin color.

Donald rolled over. "I don't mind being Godless. If He's telling people to kill other people in his name, not so good. I'll take Laughing Jesus any day."

Molly snorted. "I think the Laughing Jesus is supposed to be laughing at the stories that have been made up about him. He thinks we're taking things too seriously. Too literally. And it's a cosmic joke, humans trying to control hearts and minds of other humans."

"I can't imagine trying to explain any of this to Esme and Simon."

"Well, let's be honest," said Molly. "We can't. We can't even explain it to ourselves." Molly set her empty glass on the side table, reached to the lamp and switched it off.

God and Planets

"Ow!" ESME YELLED. Her hand went to her head. Someone had just pulled at a few hairs, hard, and they didn't leave her head.

The class bully, Wanda, was running away behind a building. She shouted: "Coon head! Get a haircut!"

It was recess, outside, an overcast day, the asphalt yard slightly damp. About a hundred kids standing or chasing around.

"Hey, Wanda," Esme chased after. "You should talk. You have *roaches* in your hair!" It wasn't far from the truth. Wanda lived in an RV outside of town, surrounded by garbage, car parts, broken lawn chairs, tires, and scattered garbage that had been pulled from plastic bags by dogs or crows. Wanda's father was one of the town drunks, her mother, a tired cleaning lady at the motel. This didn't keep Wanda from passing on the aggressions she lived with every day. She was sent home nearly once a month, and it made not a bit of difference in her habits of grabbing, punching, pulling, spitting.

Wanda was almost as marginal as Esme, yet because of her color, she felt confident picking on her. She was an insider, a "normal" person, if you just looked at color.

Esme didn't catch her. She stopped. She rubbed her head to cancel the pain on her scalp.

Soon after she was roughly bumped from behind by one of a several boys running past, chasing each other. "You're from Mars!" he shouted, blaming her for being in the way.

No I'm not, she thought. You're off by light-years. If they only knew.

The bell rang for the end of recess. They all reluctantly got behind the kids crowding the door.

It hadn't been a good morning either.

"We're going to talk about planets this morning," Miss Darling, the teacher, said. "This is the galaxy as we know it today." She pointed to a large poster, with the sun in the center, and all the planets in orbits around it. "How many of you learned there was a planet called Pluto in your first books?"

Many children nodded.

"You'll see that there is no planet called Pluto among the planets on this chart. Pluto was discovered in 1930, but then it was demoted to a 'dwarf planet' in 2006, because it was just a big snowball of ice, and it needed to have rock and ice, and be rounded due to its own gravity. That's our definition of planets. Although some are more gas than rocks."

"But isn't it big? How can we just pretend it doesn't exist?" a child asked.

"It exists. It's a large and massive object orbiting the sun. We just have some new definitions." She paused. "In fact, speaking of definitions. Did you know that there was a time when we thought that the Earth was the center of our universe?"

She paused for dramatic effect.

"Our notion changed because a Polish astronomer called Copernicus published his idea that the Sun is the center of the universe, and the planets move around it in circles. That was in 1543. Can anybody tell me how long ago that was?"

A long pause. Several students furiously scribbled. "473 years," shouted one of them, beating out the others.

"Yes, about 500 years. Copernicus based his idea on a lot of calculations and observations but he had no real proof. He waited decades to publish his theory. In fact, he died with the new book, just issued, in his hand. It took over a hundred years before astronomers were convinced. It was not accepted in his lifetime, in fact, because it contradicted the Bible. He was called a heretic by the Catholic Church, and his idea was declared wrong.

"A few people suffered mightily for trying to build on his theory. A guy named Bruno was burned at the stake for heresy, in 1600."

Esme gasped. Pleiadians were here to keep humans from tormenting each other.

"Although he was indeed a heretic on several counts. He denied the divinity of Jesus, the virginity of Mary. He denied the existence of hell, and basically, God. And he didn't have powerful friends. Galileo, who came soon after him, invented the telescope, and also discovered more evidence that the Sun was the center of the universe. He was condemned in 1633 when he was 69 years old, but he was friends with the Pope and with a Grand Duke, so they mainly put him under house arrest for the rest of his life, and his work was banned."

"Miss Darling," asked Esme, "How come people finally changed their minds and believed in the theory about the Sun, but they still believe in the divinity of Jesus, without proof?"

"That's religion, dear," she said, "The Church taught that as truth, and they never wavered."

"But Jesus might have just been a man with special powers, right? He could have gotten them from aliens, and not from God." Esme swallowed, realizing this was not the way to keep a low profile. Sherman would disapprove.

"Excuse me?" Miss Darling lowered her pointer from the chart of the planets.

"You said Copernicus, and Galileo, were eventually proven to be right. But the Church was never proven to be right." Esme now had the attention of most of the class.

"Right about what?" The teacher was frowning.

"The existence of a God. And Jesus as the son of God. Those are Church myths, like the Earth being the center of the universe."

"Esme, let's go back to science. I'll lose my job if we talk about whether God exists." She could talk about the church and history; that was different.

"I'm sorry. I just think if people are getting burned at the stake, it seems important to be sure what the truth is."

Her classmates snickered.

"Esme," the teacher said. "Esme. Planets." She turned back to the chart, and pointed, and continued naming the planets and few things about each of them.

Esme scouted the textbook for information about other celestial bodies in the sky. Finally, she found what she was looking for: the Pleiades.

"Among the nearest star clusters to Earth, and most obvious to the naked eye in the night sky." The name derives from a Greek word "to sail" because the Ancient Greek sailing season began with the annual appearance of the cluster on the horizon just before sunrise. Seven of the main stars--"hot blue"-- are named as sisters, daughters of Atlas, a Titan who held up the sky, and Pleione, the protectress of sailing. Their names are Maia, Electra, Alcyone, Taygete, Asterope, Celaeno, and Merope.

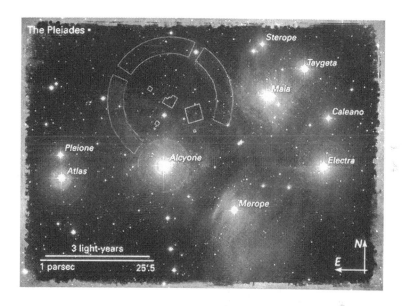

I wonder if only one of these is our home planet, she thought. We should name our vortices, she thought. Then her mind wandered trying to assign names, and she missed most of the teacher's words about planets.

The Parents

"Mom, why can't we all go back to Oregon?" asked Esme.

The two sat in the kitchen shucking fresh peas from the farmers' market that day. They had a small bushel of pea pods on the floor between them. Each of them held a big stainless-steel bowl between their knees as they took pods from a pile spilled on the table, ran a thumb through it, and caught the peas in the bowl. Empty pods were gleefully thrown into another bushel. They would make pea soup later that day, with bacon, and put containers of peas and soup into the freezer.

"Your Dad had a run-in that scared us. We got out of there, fast."

Twenty years earlier, Molly and a bunch of other hippies traveled around the Oregon backwoods visiting communes as they learned of them through word of mouth. Shopping for a spot of heaven. Molly came on a commune near Harlan, Oregon, hugging the Siuslaw National Forest, in sight of Mary's Peak, a small and relaxed mound of about 4,000 feet. The "camp" was a cluster of five old houses more like shacks about to collapse under the next rain. They called it the Secret Garden.

"We're less than fifteen people," a long-haired, skinny girl told her. "We grow our own food: tomatoes, peas, beans, potatoes. We use food stamps to get things like milk and rice in town."

A conch had just called everyone to supper, which turned out to be lentil soup, salad, and home-made bread.

A tall, skinny, gentle black boy was in the group. "I hope you decide to stay," he said, smiling.

There were no children and many dogs. Outside, chickens and a few goats. Most of the members were in their early twenties.

They gave her a mattress in a common room. After a few days as a guest, a visitor could ask to join the group. She saw the piano, a didgeridoo, and lots of guitars. People had drawn and painted on surfaces everywhere inside the house, including all over the large, mixed collection of old tables and chairs. She traveled with a sleeping bag.

The next morning, she joined the gardeners. There were people chopping wood, mending fences, going into town for part-time jobs and shopping.

"Why are you here?" she asked the black boy over dinner. Without hesitation, he came over directly to sit next to her.

"No college money. I don't want to be a slave to a menial job. How about you?"

"I want to live in the woods. Get away from the craziness going on--Vietnam, protests. I can't afford to go to school either. My parents pressure me to stay home. Be proper. Be a good girl and find a husband to support me." She had worn her best T-shirt to dinner, with a mystic eagle in a Native-American design, and a wooden-bead necklace. "What are you guys about? I mean, do you have a particular philosophy?"

"Yeah. We want minimum rules. Freedom. Everybody does what they want to do, or know how to do. Like cooking, shopping, farming. Nobody's the leader. We decide things together."

"Do you all agree?"

"No. There's a lot of talk. You have to allow for that. Somebody can feel strongly about chickens, or money. Mice in the kitchen. Whether a car repair is important." He and others spoke gently, without anger. They didn't seem to be railing against society. "We just don't want bosses. No property fights. Mutual respect. Leave each other alone. Most of us just want to coast for a while, here in the woods, and think about stuff. Put off all the rules of the game outside."

"Is the farm making it?"

"It's still early. Only a few years in. We've got a large meadow out front that could be farmed. Somebody needs to initiate that. A few of us have taken part-time jobs in town."

"Isn't that what you didn't want?"

He laughed. "It's either that or beans and rice, every day. We buy milk, butter, and such. Have to pay to keep the car running."

She knew that they hadn't asked her for anything in return for her visit. Over a few days, she could see some of the members goofing off more than others. Playing music, swimming in the creek. There was no boss to tell them to muster, get work done. Still, she decided to stay. They welcomed her hard-working style. The conversations with Donald were the most fun she'd had in years.

She learned that his genes might have come from Ethiopian stalk--graceful, smiling warriors, not her picture of Masai, who were also tall and skinny, but hard, tough, and fierce. He seemed to enjoy the Zen of kneading bread.

Donald's grandparents were part of the wave of workers--
white and black--who rushed to jobs in Portland to build ships
during the war. Almost overnight, in 1940, the Oregon Housing
Authority built about 10,000 units of wood in what became at
the time the world's biggest housing project, called Vanport.
Among the workers were about 20,000 blacks, who thus raised
the black population of Oregon by a factor of ten. The most
remarkable aspect of this was that Oregon had been created as
the only "whites only" state in the country, in 1859, with explicit
exclusionary laws against blacks. Blacks who were not resident
at that time were not allowed to come into Oregon, buy
property, or make contracts. Also among those "not welcome
here" were Japanese and Chinese people. In the 1920s, Oregon
was home to the largest Ku Klux Klan organization west of the
Mississippi, and the state legislature and governorship were
populated by KKK members. The exclusion for blacks was in the
Oregon laws into the 21st Century. Skinheads flocked to a "white
homeland" in the 1980s and 1990s.

Well, Vanport was completely wiped out by a major flood
of the Columbia River in 1948. Donald's parents moved to a
segregated section of Portland called Albina. Ship-building jobs

disappeared after the war. The exceptional indulgence of letting blacks and females work had been driven by the necessities of war, and that was over. Donald's dad became a porter for the railroad, so they were able to buy a home. But by the 1950s, Albina became a blighted slum, and soon it was subject to aggressive urban renewal that had black-owned homes cleared out to make way for a new arena, highways, and a hospital. Unable to afford college, Donald joined the young drifters heading for the woods. He sought an escape from people, all over Portland town, who fell silent when he entered a room.

He'd had a harsh lesson in the ways of exclusion, and the subtle ways of punishing whole populations that were not wanted. Equality in America was a platitude, a slogan that burned if you were black, Asian, or even white and poor.

Molly got a job in the weekly farmers market in Harlan. Donald worked part-time in a hamburger place. They biked into town and back, both glowing with health, wearing ratty clothes. Poor and free. The two started out living in corners of different houses but within months they were sharing a tiny room in one of them.

One day, Donald was late to supper. The twilight was turning dark. The group knew he had a light on his bike and could navigate the dirt road home at night. Finally, after some tension about the time, they heard him drop his bike against the wooden porch. No steps.

"Donald, are you there?" Molly got up, anxious because he was so late. She rushed out the front door to the porch. He was slumped on the steps. It was dark, but she could see there was blood on his face and hands. His jacket was torn.

"Oh my God! What happened?"

Everyone rushed out to help him up the stairs. Inside, they checked him for broken bones and cuts that might require an emergency room. His face, arms and legs were scraped from falling on gravel into a fence. His jacket had caught on the bike as he fell. But his bones were intact.

"You know that bruiser who wears leather bracelets? The big black truck? Bald head?"

They all knew him. An Aryan Nation group had moved into the area right outside Harlan too. The vast expanses of back-country Oregon had become a magnet for utopians, zealots, and white supremacists. They were only about twenty people. Everyone crossed paths in town. Their signature look was shaved heads, tattoos, piercings, guns. "He tried to run me over. Just where the dirt road starts."

"What? Why?"

"Esme." He paused and reached out to her. "He shouted that I should stay away from you." Everybody turned to her.

"No!" Esme knew the bruiser. He came to the weekly market just to flirt with her. She had no choice but to serve him, like any other customer.

"He also called me a black bastard. Not surprising." His voice was low, under control. As you would expect from a man who relaxes by kneading bread.

The bike was demolished. It was a lucky attack--the biggest scars were emotional.

There were no police in Harlan at that time. Everybody was in the countryside to get away from civilization. No police, hospitals. No authorities to keep the peace. The Secret Garden was no longer an oasis; it was too close to violent racists who seemed to enjoy their violence as a past-time.

Molly had just found out she was pregnant. She had a cousin who'd settled further up north in Washington state, near La Conner, as part of a second wave "hippy exodus" there. The cousin had raved about being near the ocean, smelling sea breezes, hearing the caw of seagulls, finding cheap land and houses. The two packed up and left the Secret Garden quickly, after spending eight years there.

Now, in Sedro Woolley, things had gone sour. Molly knew Esme was troubled by things that had happened to Simon, things that happened to her in school. Her Dad was leaving the house in the evening for long walks to cool off. They were all feeling stranger and stranger.

"We could grow our own food, Mom. You and Dad wouldn't need to make money. We could home school." Esme was up for change. She pictured an endless summer camp. "Why can' we go do that? Can't we do that?" She saw nothing inconsistent with being a Pleiadian who wanted a peaceful life. Her vibrations would reach other people and change the spiritual atmosphere of the Earth, regardless of where she lived.

"The Secret Garden never got to be self-sufficient, Esme. We lived on food stamps. We never got organized enough to expand the farm. The car was in terrible shape. We knew we were failing when it was beans and rice, week after week."

Molly leaned down to pick up the basket of shucked pea pods, got up, and emptied it into a trash can. She sat down again slowly, heavily. "I'm afraid we'll never go back to Oregon, baby."

"Why?"

"Here's the thing. You should know. Your grandparents are still in the Portland area." She shucked about ten pods. "There's a reason you've never met them."

"Huh?"

"They were really mad at your Dad when he 'went hippy' and gave up on Portland. Then they were really, really mad when he took up with me."

"Why?"

"Because we didn't get married. They're strict Baptists. They thought he shamed the family."

Esme tried to grasp the awful feeling that even family could reject you. A sense of belonging did not seem something humans valued enough. "Do they know about me and Simon?"

"I don't know. Not from us. Your Dad is pretty mad at them too. He doesn't want you to hear them say really bad things."

After another silence, Molly continued. "There's another reason we won't go back." She cleared off her apron. "You came along, and we worried about taking care of you in that environment. We needed more money, for things like doctors, a better diet. More security. Police."

"Here there's police, huh?" Esme said. "We're safe, but we have to hide from them!"

"Not hide, my dear. Live in peace." She took up Esme's finished bowl of peas.

River Cove

SIMON SAT ON THE BOARD that served as a seat in the portal that the Cabal called River Cove. It was held in place with heavy ropes on each end like a swing, except the ropes were tied short on branches in sturdy bushes. Under the seat was a three-foot bank down into the river, which at that point the flow was about five feet wide and curved, forming a deep pool. The energy of the water, flowing into the curve and out, formed a real water eddy and an energetic one, reinforced by branches that had been trained and tied to form a partial canopy. A touch of Bonsai technique, thanks to Farmer John. The whole thing was like a strange nest, nearly hanging over the water, a platform that would not be recognized by anyone as having any purpose but maybe to allow someone to observe the deep eddy below it. It was possible for a human sitting on the wide board to make it swing, maybe one foot in either direction, while holding onto branches on each side. A four-legged creature might simply hunker down and use it as a nearly-stable platform. Certain creatures they knew were capable of falling asleep on surface that unstable.

"I'm on," he said, swinging his feet a little to bounce and start some motion.

The Cabal was hunkered in the bushes behind him: Esme, Sherman, Pip, and four others. They all had to crawl on all fours to get close to the seat.

How's the water below? asked Sherman.

"Deep. The water's high today. Lots of flow," he answered.

Any fish? asked Persephone-the-Russian-blue-cat, pretending casual curiosity.

"No," he answered leaning forward for a closer look. He straightened up and then pulled on the branches to start a steady, short swing back and forth, like a metronome. He hung from his arms, relaxed, and enjoyed the hypnotic motion.

The group visited each portal periodically, to sync their own vibrations and to raise them if possible, giving them greater powers of telepathy, teleporting if necessary, and generally being a stronger presence in the so-called material world. It was the difference between being well-fed, energy-wise, as opposed to being weak and sickly. Like having a strong immune system. Not exactly a superpower but running on premium high-octane fuel.

Some years before, Farmer John discovered his favorite llama Teo dead in the field. Teo was mostly white with spots. Very old at sixteen, she mostly sat in the grassy field chewing, looking like a giant furry goose. She was one of three on the farm, and all three treated John like one of the herd: they welcomed his visits and loved hearing about his day. He told them his troubles as well, and their nurturing spirit kept him on an even keel. In fact, they were an anchor in his emotional life. Just as some men would visit a bar to relax, John stopped by for a daily chat.

Losing Teo was a blow to his heart. There she was, stretched out in a position she never held in life: head down on the grass and all four limbs stretched to the side, like a sleeping dog might lie. There was no thought of rescue at this point; he knew it was her time and she was gone. But he'd never let himself think of the moment when those big brown eyes and big overbite would not be peering at him with deep affection.

The situation posed a considerable logistical problem as well: she weighed about 300 pounds, the size of a horse. He managed to pull her body onto a tarp, and then dragged it with his tractor to a deep hole in the corner of the field, near a grove of trees. Digging the grave took him five hours of hard labor but he felt that every shovel full of dirt was a tribute to her life, and he want to give her the best effort his muscles could muster. He was sore for a few days after that untypical work, but even that reminded him of Teo, as if every sore spot and pain in his body was a smooch and a kiss from the big hunk of fur.

He pulled a log to the corner of the field to use as a bench, and he continued to visit Teo late at night when his other chores were done. Her llama sister Mabel and brother Harry did not mind, and often they came along to pay their respects too. After all, they were a mini-tribe among all the animals in the surroundings, with the special kinship that comes from being the same species.

One clear and cool night, while sitting on the bench for a one-sided chat with Teo, John saw lights come out of the sky and head toward his farm. His farm was located below a rather tall forested ridge which at night displayed a silhouette of pine trees like a decoration on a shelf against the starry sky. But, to his surprise, one or a few of those stars now appeared to charge in his direction and grow larger. He gripped the bark of this log because there was no way a plane would be flying out over his farm in the dark of night. There was no noise of helicopter blades. It was silent and as sudden as if the most powerful spotlight had been turned on and it pointed at his farm. The giant flare was not directly on him, but on a patch of woods on the far end of his property. He could not see where it hit ground because of the pitch-black forest in the way. In a second, he saw a row of colored lights hovering over the tree tops, and a beam of light below.

He jumped up to go see what was happening. He climbed over the rail fence. The darkness was no barrier for navigation-- he knew his land like the back of his hand. He'd hoed, mowed, cleared, brushed by, trampled, and stumbled through most spaces between trees and bushes. There was no direct path. The light blasted toward him making it easier to force his way toward it. When he got to the grove hosting this bizarre light festival, he saw a gigantic metallic cigar filling the space, with colors blinking along its lower rim, while below it was the glaring blaze.

A ramp came down on the right side, and something short and dark on two legs ran out of the nearby trees and up into the cigar-ship.

"Hey, hey!" John yelled.

The sound of his voice caused the ramp to lift and close quickly, with no sound. Then the whole cigar-shaped craft rose straight up in the air, slowly, clearing the trees. Then it shot straight up high in the night sky, pivoted to the right, flashed away like a shooting star, and disappeared.

It happened so fast, John might have imagined it. But he could smell something singed.

"Caroline," said John a few days later, in the cozy cocoon of her healing center, in the middle of downtown Sedro Woolley. "What's this all about? Why did that thing come to my farm? What are they after?" He'd come for a serious consultation, not just a social visit.

The room was also a shop full of crystals, flags, magic stones, scarves, and other beautiful things for sale, appealing to women who never changed their sixties ways or, recently joined the community of crones who were finally going to liberate themselves from conventions and get into their groove.

"How long have I known you?" she asked, gently.

"About five years, I think."

"I think it's time I let you in on the world as I see it."

"Well sure."

"I don't trust just anyone with it."

He raised his right palm as if taking a vow. "I want nothing but the truth," he said.

"Aliens have been visiting Earth since the beginning of our time. They started the human race, they've assisted in our evolution, in our inventions, and they check on us time to time."

"Whoa."

"Why is this a secret? Why have I only seen them once?"

"They're teleporting. Intergalactic travel. The earth is surrounded by grids of space and time, and they travel those grids. There are spectrums of light, sound, and thought. We humans are limited. We only see one octave of light. When they 'visit,' they materialize in a way that is closer to the human spectrum, and then we can see them."

"Still, in secret?"

"Our governments are afraid of an 'alien invasion.' Fear keeps them from letting people know about any witnesses who claim to have seen UFOs or aliens. You've heard all the tales of UFO's that are declared to be weather balloons, errant flights, spotlights from a distant town. It's all phony baloney."

"You mean to say there's evidence."

"There's evidence. It's suppressed. In fact, there are people who 'know too much' who disappear, along with any radar tracking data, videos, photos."

"What?!!"

"If people say they've had an experience with aliens, they lose their jobs. They're ridiculed, not questioned, or referred to some place that wants to collect information about encounters. Some of them have been traumatized because the encounter was full of fear--an instinctive response. So yes, we keep this secret."

John pulled his jacket off, settling in. "And how do they pick where they land? Who they contact?"

"There are places all over the earth that are known to have frequent UFO sightings. There are places all over the earth that have crop circles, designs left in stone, artifacts, even material left behind. These are probably places that have some significant vibration. The same way, some humans are maybe more amenable to contact, or more interesting." Caroline pointed at him, as if joking.

"Are they going to abduct me? Take samples? What?"

"I don't know, John. My intuition tells me they want something else from you. You're a builder. They want you to build some portals. Secret, of course."

"For whom? For them to come through?"

"It's two ways, John. The Earth is a very heavy dense material. They have to get through our atmosphere, and more important, our energy matrix. They come from airy places." She laughed. "Lighter places."

"And how do I do this?" John built an imaginary tower with his hands in the air.

"You build sheds, right?"

"Yes."

"You can find locations, and orientations, using dowsing rods."

"I have some copper dowsing rods."

"You're looking for spots within the cosmic grid that are like a vortex. Like a black hole someone can slip into and out of. Then you build the shed or the pyramid, or a natural spot, to focus around that spot."

"Use the dowsers."

"Yes. Ask to be led to the spots, and make it possible for earthly creatures to access it in secret. Your first spot can be my meditation shed, in the back of my house."

"Back of your house, huh? Who's going to partake of this black hole? Anybody you know doing space travel?"

"As a matter of fact, yes. You know those kids, Esme and Simon?"

"Sure. They visit my animals. Come by on bikes. They roam around a lot."

"They're part of what I call the Pleiades Cabal."

"Pleiades?"

"You know the star constellation?"

"Sure."

"Many spirits who choose to incarnate on earth as a human come by way of the Pleiades. They want to adjust to the denser material world gradually. For that, they stop at the Pleiades. It's like a Base Camp. Not for altitude. For energy and manifestation on earth."

"How many of these are there?"

"Nobody counts. Light beings are coming in from all over. But they sometimes come as part of a 'spiritual lineage.' A 'soul group.' Esme, Simon, and many of the animals around them are a team. They can talk to each other telepathically. Teo was probably among them."

"My Teo?"

"Sure. Didn't Teo calm you, and in effect 'raise your vibration?'"

"Absolutely."

"It doesn't take lectures."

"Caroline, how do you know all this?" He leaned back.

"It's part of my mission. We all have different paths. Mine included wakening Esme, Simon, Sherman, Bailey, the cats, the crow, and other creatures to their Pleiadian roots. They need to practice raising their vibrations so they can visit the fifth dimension. They already see spirits, for example. It's quite a large community, when you think about it." She reached over to him. "And you can help. Give them places to make it easier to experience other dimensions. Possibly teleport. They're learning who they are."

"How will I know I've built the thing right? Do you have a test?"

"Ask the dowsers. They'll tell you. You could also try the portal yourself. It's like a window. Or a doorway to another dimension." She chuckled. "Be careful it's not a one-way ticket."

"That's my mission?"

"It seems to fit who you are and who you're becoming. Welcome to the Cabal!" She straightened a bright mirrored cloth on the table beside her. "The Earth was intended to become a magnificent, intergalactic center for the exchange of information. Information is beamed to us. Our bodies must be able to receive it and beam it back out to others. We're like radio stations."

"And do I talk to these friends telepathically?"

"You can try. As your vibrations change, you synchronize. Just like the aliens synchronize to us for contact. The Cabal will know you've joined us. But you can tell them to go try out any portals." She paused. "We're trying to become multi-dimensional beings, awaken our DNA, raise our frequency, be able to interact with extraterrestrial light-bearing energies.

"You know, Caroline, one of my neighbors had an uncle who built shacks along Hansen Creek, where the Bug House

116

patients went to relax. There were people said to 'have spells' when they went out on the goat and logging trails."

"There you go."

"And you've heard of the white-breasted swallows that arrive in a giant swarm at the campus every spring, and depart in September. They're like a magical blessing on the place. Something unique to this area."

"I wish I'd seen them. Please remind me if they're still doing that, when it's time."

Caroline got up and went to make them tea. John leaned back and rested his eyes. And his brain, probably.

"You might even see Teo again, John," she said, setting a cup of tea next to his arm. "She might look like a fuzzy light, but you'll know by the way you feel."

"That would be nice."

"She did lead you to the tribe, you know."

And here in the present, the Cabal sat watching Simon who sat on a little platform over the River Cove portal. He rocked a few more times, and then his form evaporated as if it were a puff of smoke all along. Leaving Nothing on the platform. The wooden board still swayed a little and then came to rest, since there was no weight on it to serve as a pendulum.

This had never happened before. The rest of the Cabal were silent.

"He's gone," said Esme, almost to herself.

Gone, said Sherman.

Gone, said Pip.

Gone, said Bailey.

"He'll be back, right Sherman?" Esme turned to him.

I think so, said Sherman. *If he's skipped out of this time or this place, there is no time to go by. You know what I'm saying?* He sounded a little hesitant which was totally out of character.

"I want him back. We're not used to this. Who's going to fetch him back?"

Not me, said Pip.

Not me, said Bailey.

Let's take a nap in the grass over here, said Sherman. *Take a break. It's still sunny out. We're safe. Okay?*

They retreated from the dense undergrowth next to the creek to a patch of tall grasses behind them. It may have been their first group nap. They tried to let the warm sunshine put them at ease.

Esme woke up with tears in her eyes. "I want him back," she sat up and looked for Sherman. There he was, a few feet away, his thick body pancaked on his belly, back legs stretched straight behind him, big floppy ears touching the ground, around a resting snout. "Sherman. Who can help us?"

Maybe Farmer John. We're just back of his house. Maybe he's there.

"Let's go. Okay?" She rolled over onto her knees. It felt like they'd been waiting a long time. The group had taken a nap in the hot sun, which relieved their tension, but now they realized he wasn't back and got worried.

John was also known as John the Shed Builder. He was actually a carpenter, handy-man, and electrician who lived on a 40-acre farm. When people wanted a retreat shed, or an artist studio, or a storage locker for gardening gear, or a meditation room, or a playhouse, they called on John to build it. He was creative and fast, and Sedro Woolley was littered with his structures. They were mostly small, the kind that didn't need a permit, since they had no electricity or plumbing. Really, less than ten by ten feet foundation. He used any materials people wanted, sometimes scavenging old windows, doors, even VW busses, to customize with paint and other finishings. In fact, it was now a fad to have a "dream cabin in the back" if you were anybody with a few thousand dollars to spare for such an outrageous luxury. Plenty of those people in Sedro Woolley too.

John had known Caroline from nearly the day she arrived. In fact, he'd been a client of hers, getting a reading on his status in the universe. Things he needed to get over. Improvements in his attitude. Tasks he might assume. Some of the "whys" and "whats" of his life's journey so far. He was an unassuming, gentle, skinny man with gray hair and beard, wearing sandals, jeans, a plaid wool shirt, maybe a simple dark knit hat to warm his thinning scalp. People wanted a lot from him, in the way of repairs and fixes to their houses and farms, but he did not rush to satisfy them. They had to wait for his deliberate, careful handiwork. On his terms. He never hired anybody to help him. Some of his competitors hated the fact that he did nothing to hype up business. He had no hustle. But he didn't need any to have enough work to do. His brand was trust and reliability. Not to mention, a low mercenary impulse.

What most of the human community didn't know was that John had made some of the structures into a portal for the Cabal. The sheds or customized RV's had a loose board or such through which members could squeeze, and then conduct business that might need shelter from prying eyes, and sometimes shelter from unpleasant elements. Business like stepping into another dimension for a bit. Ha ha

It was a rule that members could leave no poop inside, even if they did not like the shed owner. They practiced the hiker's rule: no impact, no evidence. Now, there was some discussion about human allergies to fur that could cause a reaction when the owners came back into their shed during the day, but fur-bearing members of the Cabal were advised to stay on their feet and hang onto their hair! So far, so good.

The sheds were part of a sacred geography for the Cabal. It included places within the Bug House compound, large cedar tree stumps like Cedar Canyon that once served as small homes in early Sedro Woolley history (after the lumber industry took down giant trees), Tibetan Cave in a rock cliff, and River Cove. There was Great Pyramid, on John's property, which was simply a four-sided lumber frame, but surrounded by dense trees. Also, Forest Maze, used when someone needed to ratchet up a complex vortex effect. It was a place no non-participating human would detect, because the path through the maze was guided by certain plants that would indicate turning points in the maze. Thank you, Sedro Woolley, for wild untamed woods, even if some of them were owned by an absentee urban landlord who was twenty years from retirement and held the land as a

future dream scenario. Truly, these were multi-use lands, whether you knew it or not!

In the Cosmic Grid

No ONE TOLD THE CABAL WHAT HAPPENED when you entered a vortex, which is like a black hole. Caroline forgot to mention that there was an invisible time/space cosmic grid formed by a cazillion stacked pyramid spaces that filled the entire universe. Every unit of energy had a "station" at many intersections all over it -- representing past lives, current parallel lives, future lives, non-Earthly lives, and dwellings in spirit and animal form. People intersect with each other and with everyone they ever knew and ever will know, many times, all over this grid. People echo our other energy versions through deja vu, sometimes.

"Pleiadians are time jumpers," said Caroline. Could be confusing.

The instant Simon disappeared through the vortex, he found himself in the dark, on a wooden veranda over a narrow cobble-stone street. He hovered, sitting in the shadows between two wooden buildings, near a large wooden door. Above him was a white-screened window with a clean dark wooden grating over it, which he recognized as Japanese. Opposite him was a long wooden wall with dark vertical boards, ending under a steep thatched roof. He was watching for the door to open, for people to exit, giving him a chance to creep through the door, unseen, in the dark.

He was still a boy, but cold and hungry. Inside the door was the kitchen of a barely-surviving, rustic Butoh theater and school. He'd lived off the food left on plates moved to the kitchen for cleaning: rice balls, morsels of fish, sea vegetables, and tofu pieces. The place was understaffed and the room thus empty for long periods of time. It was warmer than outside. He had to resist the temptation to dwell near the wood-burning stove, where coals were kept glowing all day and night.

It was more than food that kept him in this place. He loved watching the Butoh rehearsals. Butoh portrayed the misery and grotesqueness of extreme environments, like skid rows, cemeteries, caves. The misery of people like Simon-the-Japanese-urchin. By tradition, the Butoh acolytes deprived themselves of comfort as part of their training. They practiced grimaces, silent screams, clawed hands, rolled-up eyes, and physical contortions usually made by people in agony. This he found comforting because it legitimated his existence--he too was an apprentice to the Misery. He even hoped for admission to the inner sanctum of the school, some day. He was an orphan sharing a hovel with street people who had to hide from authorities because they posed the opposite of the esthetics that Japanese people prized: a clean, beautiful, calm, precise composition. Skid rows were not sanctioned neighborhoods. They were always on the verge of being demolished, with no mercy to the dwellers.

Today he found a plate of generous portions hastily placed on a counter near the stove. Possibly the owner meant to finish it later. He grabbed the fried fish and stuffed his mouth, his other hand reaching for rice balls to put in his pocket. His cheeks were bulging with the strain of over-sized bites. His eyes watered with pleasure and relief: another day without hunger pangs.

"OW!" he cried, feeling the sting of a switch on his back. He knew it; it was kept in the kitchen for precisely the purpose of beating him away. "Ma!" he cried, a general appeal to help, a generic "Ma." He held his full pocket closed with one hand and scrambled toward the door on all fours. "OW!" the switch struck again.

"Get out of here, you urchin! If I catch you again, you'll not forget the beating!"

A giant claw-like male hand grabbed the back of his dirty cotton shirt.

"Stop!" they both heard in the direction of a door to the back of the stage. The hand on his back tightened on the cloth while both of them looked up.

There stood a young woman, made up for rehearsal.

"Leave that boy! He's just hungry!" she exclaimed.

Simon-the-urchin used the opportunity of the distraction to pull away, hard. His shirt ripped off his back. Even in the dim light his naked back was visible: frail and emaciated. His body looked even smaller with the stark appearance of a long narrow birth mark. It looked like he'd been sliced open with a sword.

She screamed as if her own life was about to be taken. It was an authentic Butoh pose of torment: a woman in agony, screaming, but not silently.

Simon used all four limbs to exit through the door. He disappeared into the night behind the theater.

The woman fell to the floor into a physical contortion. The cook was frozen in shock, a ragged piece of shirt clutched in his hand. He didn't know it, but she'd had a baby boy stolen from her when she was too young to be bearing a child. He was born with a strange reddish-blue stripe on his back, which she saw when the old doula pulled him out of her hands.

Back at the River Cove, the cabal picked themselves up from the grass. They formed a solemn, silent parade in the direction of John's farmhouse. They crossed a long field, a crude wooden bridge over a little creek, through a few fence gates, then a dirt road to the house. His truck was gone. No one answered at the house.

"Sherman," Esme spoke.

How about you go find Simon, said Sherman.

"We've never done that before." She frowned. "Is it even possible?"

Caroline said you could manifest anything.

"Yeah, but the grid. What's my map?"

Your will, my dear. Your will.

"Will you come and find me if I get lost?"

Of course. We'll all just pitter-patter about on the grid and pray our pinky-finger bonds bring us together. Sherman did the dog equivalent of heh-heh. *Oh wait, I don't have a pinky finger.*

Esme teared up. "You're making fun. Simon is lost! Sherman!"

*Now, now. Esme. I have full confidence. Let's use the pyramid.
That's the strongest portal.*

She wiped her face with her shirt.

They formed a silent parade to the back field that held the
wooden pyramid. It was about six feet tall, nestled between
trees. John kept the interior base cropped close, making it look
like a decorative sculpture.

Esme sat inside the structure with the Cabal surrounding
the structure as if a performance was about to begin. She barely
heard the *Ohhhhhhh* around her as she felt a whoosh and a
lightness in her body that she'd never felt before.

After she disappeared through the vortex, Esme felt as if
she'd just been sucked through a vacuum tube, the kind they
used to have in banks. She checked her body. She was wearing
a thick wool sweater over a long wool skirt, and an apron. She
was at a bench in a room that looked like a cross between a
gardener's and a cook's den. There were herbs in bundles all
over a very long wooden table. Herbs were hanging overhead in
drying bundles. There was a stove at the other end of the room,
with pots sending up aromatic steam. Along the opposite wall
were little jars that weren't canned fruits. They were more like
extracts, with labels written in a neat small hand. She was
making new bundles by sorting herbs from two big baskets on
the table in front of her.

Her mother came in to check the stove. She wasn't a slight
woman but seemed strong by the way she moved. Her woolen
skirt swished as she walked across the room. She had graying
hair, and wore a woolen shawl over her shoulders, tied and
secured out of the way in her waistband. Her hands were like
the hands of an angel: delicate, light, almost fluttering instead of

moving. Esme knew their magic touch on her forehead when she had a fever, on her head when her mother leaned over to caress her.

"I've sent a message in a basket of eggs, to the camp. We have no way of knowing if he got it. We have to have faith that he did," she said, when Esme-the-farm-girl looked up expectantly.

They were peasants in a Northern Baltic forest. The Imperial Russians were in control of the countryside. They had just started a war with Japan, and they needed cannon-fodder. Peasants were perfect. They already raided their farms for horses, cattle, grains, and produce, and now they harvested men with good backs. The recruits were being trained on another farm about five miles away. The local women and old men supplying the garrison tried to bring news both ways. The Russian soldiers thought nothing of shooting anyone on the slightest pretext.

Esme's mother was a medicine woman and this held no special privilege in the eyes of the authorities. Officers and soldiers would sneak their way to her house for remedies: burns, cuts, broken bones, infections. But there was no sense of loyalty, even toward a healer. They themselves would be shipping out to the front, and the hell with anyone anywhere, at this point. Just following orders. The regional bosses were busy, simply counting bodies conscripted and bodies loaded onto trains for the Eastern Front, trying to meet their quotas. Tsar Nicholas II was going to defend the honor of his Empire regardless.

That night, the two of them bundled up bread, cheese and sausage. They put on heavy woolen coats. The mother hooked their tired old horse to a wagon. After dark they set out on an overgrown path with two ruts for wheels that served as a

128

country road. The wagon wheels wobbled but that had been true for a long time. After several miles, they approached a forest in which the recruits were sent, with guards, to gather wood.

Since the Russian soldiers felt little loyalty to anyone and felt like victims themselves, they could be bribed to do a bad job of guarding. A bottle of lemon vodka, home-brewed, was worth more than gold.

The wagon pulled up to a familiar outcropping of rocks and stopped. Esme's mother got out and walked toward the back of the rock. It was also possible that an angry soldier could simply shoot the bearer of gifts and collect his booty, scot-free. One had to pray for a spot of integrity and honor, and humanity. It was nearly pitch dark but farmers in that area had a certain night vision, used to finding the tiniest of reflections of star light to guide their way. Esme sat trembling on the wagon seat. Her instructions were to take the reins and strike the horse into action on the slightest suspicion of failure. She was only eight years old and that was old enough for brutal men.

She heard a rustle in the bushes. Her shivers turned into hard shakes. She barely held onto the reins.

"Sweetie." Esme heard a whisper. Her mother's hand was on the side of the wagon. Then her other hand appeared. Then she pulled herself into the seat beside Esme. "Shhhh," she said, having felt her daughter's cold, shaking hands as she took the reins.

She gently coaxed the horse to move forward, slowly, to minimize the creaking of the wagon as it moved.

Esme took her mother's arm, leaned into the wool and cried without making a sound.

After a few miles, heading away from their home, her mother leaned over to her. "It's good, my dear," she said, stroking Esme's wet cheek with her butterfly fingers. Then she leaned back in the seat, and reached a hand behind her. A man's hand came up from the tarps in back, and took hers.

They drove the wagon another ten miles in the middle of the night, where Esme-the-farm-girl's father got out, took the bundle of food, and transferred to another waiting wagon. It was a piece of the Baltic underground railroad. The network would take him to a train eventually to Bremen, and a ship to America. Mostly Jews had created the secret network of hand-offs, as Jews fled Russian pogroms for decades. But they accommodated the rush of men escaping conscription. They didn't know it, but more than 100,000 men would be lost in the Russo-Japanese War, and there would be no memorials to those forced to give their lives. They were prisoners, victims, not a loyal army.

Esme and her mother made do with their modest farm. Her mother's weekly healing clinics were well attended, by people traveling from as far as fifty miles to visit her, and they bartered food, chickens, pigs, flour. In fact, the two almost flourished in this invisible economy and health care system.

Six months later, a farmer came by from the north. He joined a small group of people waiting for consultations. In about an hour, his turn came. Esme's mother was in the main room of their cottage, at a table--her "clinic," where she had her most common remedies. The man sat down heavily and leaned toward her. Esme was putting logs into the wood-burning stove. She saw her mother collapse. She jumped up and ran to her.

"What? What?" she looked at the man, still in his coat, holding his hat as if in mourning.

"Your father. The boat went down," he said.

Esme screamed and screamed. "No! No!"

Her father's middle name was Simon.

Now, suddenly, a flash to another reality. In a climate that seemed hot and dusty, Esme was bending down to drink water from a stream in the early morning. She was wearing deer skins and moccasins. She was tired and dirty. She heard a noise, startled, and picked up a rock.

There was a Navajo Simon! In buckskins, an older version of himself, across the creek, also huddled low as if hiding. He looked ecstatic to see her and motioned for her to stay silent. As her older brother, he had raised her and taught her all the skills a Navajo needed to survive in the wilderness.

Both his hands went up facing her, then he lowered them and directed them slowly toward her. It was a blessing, just in case. Then he held his right hand open toward her, fingers spread, and turned it slightly two or three times. This was "How are you?"

She returned the blessing gesture.

He pointed to a sandy surface opposite to her and moved toward her. She crouched and crossed the little creek on a few rocks and joined him.

"I am so glad you're alive," he said. He knelt beside her and put his hand on her arm. It was customary to avoid direct eye contact.

"I nearly didn't make it," she said.

She told him about a raid on the village by government soldiers, on horses, to pick up children for the missionary school. They were sweeping Navajo villages in order to baptize and "civilize" the "heathens." They would be given haircuts, forbidden to speak their language, and have their real names replaced. Totally under the power of "god-fearing" types, they might be subjected to various abuses by ideologues.

The only way to escape capture was to run, and hope for refuge with another village. To be a visible, free-ranging child in a Navajo village was hazardous.

Esme had escaped the raid. She wasn't able to bring anything with her--jerky for food, a knife, a spear for fishing. Simon was away from the village. He had managed to avoid capture for three years now, and was often away hunting, so he was no longer visible when the surprise raiders arrived. Now they couldn't return because they were going to be hunted.

"Do you know if they're following you? Do they know which way you ran?" he asked.

"Yes. They saw me in the hills behind the village. That much."

"Then we need to go to the valley as fast as possible. There are caves there."

He got up, and they ran like deer through the brush in the direction of a deep valley, miles away. He knew animal tracks throughout the whole area and this made them able to move fast, but once they got to the plateau over the valley, they would be visible.

They were spotted just a mile from the steep cliffs they needed to descend into the valley. They could hear horses and shouts nearly half a mile away.

The soldiers caught up with them right at the edge of the plateau. They were cornered. One of the horsemen dismounted and came at them with a sword. He was furious to be outwitted by heathen children. He was determined to either capture or kill them--they were evidence of his shame.

Navajo-Simon took Esme's hand, squeezed it hard, and said, "We're going to jump." As he said that, he felt a sword slice down his back diagonally. It couldn't go deep, however, because they were nearly in the air at the time. Below them, a raging river marked the bottom of the canyon. There would be no climbing to a cave.

The two of them woke to a familiar place--at least a place they'd been before, together! They were sitting on the swing over the River Cove portal, side by side. Their faces looked as if they were mid-air in a death fall. Their expressions were totally incongruous with the River Cove setting: the gentle breeze, the sunshine, the sound of buzzing insects, the sound of a gentle creek. Just seconds ago, things were different.

Aaaahhhhhh, said a couple of Cabal members staring at them. *Finally!* They'd returned to a vigil beside the River Cove in hopes that Simon would come back where he'd made his exit. To their relief and surprise, both kids came back at the same time.

Esme flipped herself backwards off the swing. She laughed. "I found you!"

Caroline and Her Cave

A FEW YEARS EARLIER, Caroline told Esme, "Your Mom was a big help to me when I came to Sedro Woolley." They sat in her meditation shed sipping hot tea, in colorful ceramic mugs that they'd brought from the house. Windows on all sides gave the place the feel of a glass box in the woods. Trees surrounded it, hiding a view of the main house and anything beyond thirty feet away in the direction of fields and forest beyond. Even squirrels and chipmunks barely noticed there were people in the glass box as they scurried about. Sitting inside was like being inside everyday forest life: quiet, green. Only they were dry. Especially dry, inside the woods of the Northwest, was sweet.

"How so?" asked Esme.

"I came here directly from Nepal. I was bone-skinny from a meager nun's diet and a simple life style. I knew I wanted to start a shop here, but I had nothing but the address of a room where I could stay, and money that had been sitting in my bank account for quite a long time."

"How'd you know you wanted to be here?"

"I had a grandfather who came here to work the lumber. He had stories about the forests, the rivers, Mount Baker. It seemed magical. He didn't live very long because the work was really hard. But the stories he told sounded like he thought he was in heaven. I'd never been here before, myself."

"You wanted it because he liked it?"

"Right. His spirit told mine to just skip all the other places. Jump right in."

"And Mom?"

"Your Mom and Dad were already here. Simon was just born. Your Dad avoided the usual cheap labor jobs. He found work at the bakery early on, and luckily, it's been a long-lasting business and he's gotten along there. Your Mom was trying to take care of you on a very low income. She would get away when she could, to come to yoga class. That's where we met."

"Yoga class? In Sedro Woolley?"

"Now you're talking like an outsider. Of course. I have to admit, I started the classes. But yoga was already a fad. You had yogis bringing it here from India back in the 1960s. Then it got to be mainly a form of healthy exercise, separate from Hinduism. Although we continue to use a lot of the Hindu words. It's not so much of a religious practice now."

"And Mom took your class?"

"Yes. It was popular. All the hippies that came up from Haight Ashbury, all the people like your parents that came out of the woods of the Northwest. It was a magnet. Like a party in a strange land!" She laughed. "We were hippy ex-pats!"

"My parents came out of the woods?"

"Well they were in a commune in Oregon for many years. Did you know that?"

"Oh. Yes. Mom told me." Esme the 12-year-old was already in control of a few facts.

"I love your Mom. You know that. But all of us had some rocky roads on the way."

"So. Your story?"

"I bought my shop, with space for a yoga studio in back. I hired your Mom to help me set it up. Paint, go buy some used furniture. Put up signs. We clicked."

"She worked for you?"

"No. She did a few jobs for me. I couldn't afford an employee. But she started sending me clients for readings. We started a book club. She got me into the community."

"Do people think you're a witch?"

"Esme! Where'd you get that?"

"School. Parents talking. They don't understand what you do."

"Yes. That's a problem. You would think there would be enough of us around here to make people a little more familiar. All us old hippies! But some people never get away from their strict church. And for them, the devil's always just around the corner." Caroline laughed. She was more than an old hippy. Pleiadians were just not recognized as a sub-culture. Ha ha.

"I went to Bible school one summer," said Esme. "They wanted me to get 'saved.' I didn't understand 'saved' from what?"

"Saved from your sins. They think you're born a sinner. And God the Father has to bless you, and save you from hell, where you will go if you are a sinner."

"But what did I do, to sin?"

"Nothing. Except that you were born. Jesus is right there. Waiting to save you."

"But you said we're all part of The Source."

"Yes. That's our religion. That there's no big male God out there to whom we pray. We're here as pieces of energy, manifest in the third dimension, and every one of us is creating the world, in every dimension, simultaneously, across all time."

"Isn't that nicer than being a sinner? Why don't people like that? Who wants to be a sinner?"

"The old male-God-believing religions want sinners. All over the world. They have priests that need to be serviced. They have soldiers. Where would they be if you said to a priest: 'you're the same as me.' That would be blasphemy."

"What makes them so mean?"

"They think that they're making people better. More saintly. Pure. But they're coaching you into obedience. All the big religions--Christian, Muslim, Jewish, Mormon--want power over people. They think that their idea of a good society is the only one. They each have a different idea about what's a saintly society. But I'll tell you, all of them, in their extreme forms, put women into a little box. And punish women if they try to climb out."

"What box?"

"They try to make you think that you're impure, that you're mentally inferior. You're only good for babies and housework. A slave of sorts, except it's 'God's plan' for you. Your holy place in life."

"Is that why you didn't have kids?"

"No. I don't have kids because I couldn't see how I could nurture kids and seek enlightenment the way I wanted to. There are, however, Buddhist nuns who were mothers." Caroline re-braided her hair falling down her chest.

"You were a nun?"

"I was a nun-like person. I changed my mind about living in a cave and thinking about making myself into a super spiritual creature. I came here!"

"You didn't like it?" Esme hadn't had many caves in her life. The one they called the Tibetan Cave, that John had made into a vortex, was the only cave in her life. It wasn't a place you could live.

"I like people more than being alone in a cave. I decided that I like the crazy deal of being an imperfect human, with some bad karma, and being a human that really tries to serve others and helps build the spiritual vibration of everybody, not just myself. Trying to be a good person around other people is a noble thing, too."

Most people could not imagine spending years alone, much less being alone in so much discomfort, meditating. Yogis did it all the time. They were mentally transcending mundane life and interactions with people, to concentrate their minds on spiritual states.

"Should I think of trying out the cave?" Esme admired Caroline and took it for granted that this was a good thing.

"No, Esme. You're a Pleiadian. You're an energy within a cabal that can catalyze growth in all sentient beings. Working communally is more fun. It's just as challenging too. But we're like Guardians of the Earth here. The evil we fight oppose is ignorance, meanness, greed. We try to foil the worst instincts that occur in the energies residing in a human or animal body. I guess we have our own definition of who's a sinner! And our own notion of what it means to be 'saved' from being a stupid destructive beast. Saved from being just plain mean to others. And destroying the earth."

"But we don't have priests."

"Certainly not. Our wisest spiritual guide is ourselves, inside. Our own 'higher self.' You are your own priest. I am my own priest. We are each a piece of the Source. There are no churches that need our money, and often more and more over time. There is no tithing, no emerald altars, no predatory priests, no nuns 'punishing' unwed mothers. No men gathering to stone a woman to death for disobeying them or for questioning the little box they have in mind for her. Basically, attacking her because she's a woman, and not a man. No stoning. I don't want to tell you all the perversions of punishments that humans do in the name of God. Maybe we should make a quilt of them! Your Mom makes quilts!" She smiled to soften the message. A twelve-year-old, a novice Pleiadian-on-Earth, was too young for the worst faces of the human race.

What Caroline didn't explain was that when she was in the cave, she "saw" her identity as a Pleiadian. After her extreme long meditation in the cave, she could recognize other Pleiadians, which proved true when she came to Sedro Woolley. Some of them turned out to assume animal form, in this life, like Sherman. Part of her mission was to help other Pleiadians remember their identity, too.

Caroline's Sister

MOLLY, ESME AND SIMON WERE OUTSIDE IN THE YARD trimming bushes and weeding as part of their fall clean-up when a car pulled up. A stocky woman, in a tank top and blooming cotton shorts, barely took time to slam the car door as she jumped out and stormed toward them. She was flush, maybe from the exertion, her slip-on sandals barely keeping up with her feet. A man was far behind her, heavier, slower. They could hear feet tearing through the tall grass.

"Are you Molly?" she barked, barely within hearing distance. "Are you Molly?" She stumbled, looking ahead, not paying attention to her feet. Much of her hair had escaped a ponytail and battered her eyes as she walked.

"Yes." Molly got up from the ground, easing her knees into standing. She pulled her shirt down slowly and carefully, as if she were trying it new, on in front of a mirror. Still wearing dirty gardening gloves.

"I'm Jackie, Caroline's sister," the woman sputtered with barely a pause, "We just came from Garrison's office." She finally reached them near the bushes, her feet wet from dewy grass.

Molly straightened up. Esme was about fifteen feet away, wielding long-bladed clippers.

"That house is mine. I must have it." Jackie had her hands on her hips. The hair was an inadequate shield over her eyes.

"I'm sorry," said Molly. "Please slow down."

"You're not kin. Caroline's house is mine." The woman folded her arms.

"But it was left to me, I'm afraid. There's a will." Molly tried a sympathetic smile.

"Will, schmill. That's just wrong." By now, the heavy man had caught up but stood a few feet away as if leaving room for a skirmish. His cropped head was streaming sweat, and a green cotton shirt with the tails out was soaked in big patches. His sneakers were strained out of shape and also soaking wet from the short walk.

"Caroline said you hadn't seen each other in thirty years. You didn't seem that close," Molly said.

"Blood is thicker than water. Whatever. I need that house. We need that house," Jackie sputtered.

"She needs the house," said the man. He didn't seem to know what to do with his arms that hung away from the bulk of his body.

"It's not a question of need, is it," said Molly, calmly. Esme kept holding the clippers, blades up, frozen in position, riveted.

"We have debts. I want that house."

"Caroline said that you went to Hawaii and Las Vegas last year. Can't be that bad."

"Nick needs his breaks. He deserves his breaks. Anyway, it's none of your business." Her hand with bright red-painted long nails pawed hair away from her eyes.

"Jackie." Molly took her gloves off, slowly, a technique she'd learned in her experience with difficult customers in the market. "I'm sorry."

"Sorry! You betcha. I'm coming after that house."

"The will says if you contest, you get nothing. Check with Garrison."

A mean look took over Jackie's sweaty face. She looked as if she could hit somebody, and as if she'd done it before.

Simon was up in a tree nearby, behind the bushes. He looked down as if he were watching a show in a theater. He didn't seem worried, just amazed at the drama.

"Come on, Jackie." Nick reached for her arm. He finally had a use for his arm.

She brushed him away. "You're all godless witches," she shouted, "and I mean that with a B."

The two turned away and tripped back through tall grass toward their car. Calico cat sat nearby, observing, and dodged a sandaled foot that took a gratuitous sweep at him, a near miss.

"Esme, I'm sorry," Molly said.

"How can that be your fault," Esme said. "Were they really sisters?"

"Hard to see how they came out of the same childhood. I think they both ran away from home as soon as they could. In different directions." Molly took a deep breath. "If it weren't for DNA, they would have had nothing to do with each other."

"Do you really have Caroline's house?" asked Esme.

"Yes," said Molly, "And we need it too. We're going to move there. Dad's going to stay here." She pushed her muddy hands back into the crusty cloth gloves, with several fingers more than peeking through on each hand, and knelt back down to pull weeds.

Esme looked up at the tree, midway, where Simon was sitting on a heavy branch. His chin leaned into his hands, which were wrapped around a branch in front of him, holding on.

Molly kept a flood of thoughts to herself as she grabbed weeds. These were things too adult for her to share with Esme. Caroline had told her about her righteous sister Jackie, a fierce evangelical, who with her husband spouted "get government out of my face" and yet who managed to collect every benefit they could weasel, sometimes with lies and fake job injuries. Nick was a gun nut who railed against everyone, feeling that he was a victim of oppression. He lost jobs very quickly after starting them and never questioned himself. He and Jackie had never earned as much as they spent. Jackie had moved in with her mother to help her in her final years, but when she moved in, she brought unemployed Nick, and all three lived off of Mom's Social Security. Jackie had violent incidents with Nick, but neither quit the deadly embrace of their mutual dependency. Nick and Jackie were united in their anger against the world for not handing them an easy ride, and spite and disdain for Caroline and her lifestyle. Caroline's mother was too weak to temper it. Caroline's distance from them was the only way she could avoid their hostility, and avoid the aggravation of watching "takers" exploit her mother. After their mother died, leaving the house to Jackie, the couple squandered any profits within six months.

These stories brought Molly and Caroline to a shared point of view that some people will never change, and you have to give up trying for any rapport with them. You have to find and secure your niche apart from them, and build a wall around that niche to keep them out.

Molly was too shaken to think about Esme and Simon right now. Some of Caroline's baggage was her baggage now, but it weighed on all of them, really.

UFO Sighting

RAYMOND SHARPSHRIFTER, THE EDITOR of the *Sedro Sentinel,* was blessed with the news of a UFO sighting south of town over the top of a low ridge you could call the foothills of the Cascades. He got a phone call one morning from a farmer who prided himself on living "off the grid" and deep in the woods. In fact, it was a bold move for this citizen to give up his privacy, and drive his beaten old truck down to a place in range of a cell phone tower.

"Ray, I think we're getting invaded by aliens. You've got to sound the alarm. Is anybody even prepared for this?" he shouted into his phone over a poor connection.

"Say what?" asked Ray.

"Aliens. A UFO landed on the ridge behind me last night. I've got my shotgun, but it might not be enough. You need to send reinforcements."

"Reinforcements for what?"

"Alien invasion. Aliens. They're coming down. Ray. Can you hear me?" the caller pleaded.

"Who is this, and can I come and talk to you?" Ray made some notes and closed up the office. It was only about ten miles away. The caller was going to wait at an intersection off of Highway 530. Could be a crazy, but the story was ripe for attention.

As it turns out, the caller was enjoying a toke of marijuana, perfectly legal in Washington state, on his back porch facing the ridge, when a circle of lights the width of a football stadium descended over the ridge. From beneath that circle emerged small flying lights that headed out in different directions. They danced in the black space of the sky like large moving stars, at times forming a pattern like a triangle, and then they would disappear in a blink. Finally, the large circle of larger colored lights, surrounding what looked like black hole but was possibly the space ship blocking a patch of starry night, lifted slowly, pivoted diagonally north, and itself disappeared in a blink. The caller was too frightened to hike up the ridge. In fact, he slept with his shotgun pointed at the door of his shack.

Sharpshrifter placed the story on the front page of the *Sentinel*, with a drawing of the UFO, possibly embellished for dramatic effect. He called Officer Kameron to check if there were any authorities that would be sent to investigate. There were none, unless there was evidence of unlawful activity. It was not against the law to fly your UFO over that particular ridge, at that time, he told Sharpshrifter. (Ha ha!)

Sharpshrifter called on UFOlogists anywhere to come an investigate. It might put Sedro Woolley on the map, at least for a short news cycle. He knew they were out there after he'd searched on UFO sightings and found that there were people like storm chasers whose hobby was to make a record of sightings.

"UFO? Or Mystery Lights?

A strange sight appeared to a citizen living south of Sedro Woolley in the vicinity of highway 530 and Oso: lights around the rim of gigantic flying saucer over a forested ridge. Anyone else see it? Of course, it could be a nighttime mirage or a hallucination, but we welcome witnesses. Contact the editor."

Traffic along highway 530 increased for a few weeks. The ridge over the alleged area was steep and not a place even casual hikers would tackle. The ground was unstable, and deforestation made it risky.

Esme often performed the service of delivering her mother's home-made essential oils to people's homes in the radius surrounding Sedro Woolley. She enjoyed the adventure of finding a new location. She always got a joyous response from the recipient, usually an older woman who had visited Caroline's shop in town and learned of a particular potion that might ease arthritis pain, a sore that wouldn't heal, or just a touch of nausea. The region was of course full of herbs growing naturally in the wild, if you knew where to find them, and Molly had a reputation for making good stuff.

"This is not a short distance," her mother warned. "Are you up to ten miles each way?" She knew the area was safe because it was populated by farms that avoided paved roads and traffic.

"I know back ways in that direction, Mom. There are even deer trails that will cut that distance by a lot." Donald and Molly had raised independent, resourceful kids. They were one notch above survivalists. One good thing about Sedro Woolley was their social network of kindred spirits and kind people, many connected through classes at Caroline's center.

Esme set out on her bike, avoided main roads and threaded the fields and backwoods as much as her bike could handle. About five miles in, on the edge of a forest, far away from a road, she stopped to drink water and eat her granola bar. It was mid-day, sunny, and she could smell the greenery drying out in the sun. She wasn't sure, but something else made her stop just right there.

From behind a tree, a figure came out, looking like something Esme had never seen before: seven feet tall, flowing blond hair, blue eyes, pale skin, wearing robes like an angel. The eyes and skin seemed lit from inside. Luminous, but not scary luminous. Telepathically, Esme heard: *Wait, my dear. Listen.*

Esme relaxed. She intuited that the female figure was an actual Pleiadian. Caroline had told her they actually came to earth sometimes, in spite of the difficulties of putting on the "suit" of a properly-appearing body.

You need to turn back. It's not safe. The humans in this area have abused it and destabilized it. They will suffer consequences.

"Wow," said Esme, telepathically. "Right now? What about Mrs. Taylor? She's just a few miles away."

She's been called into town. You need to turn back. Now. The woman--an angel, a fairy, a mirage?--turned back to the tree beside her. She walked, or rather flowed, as if unsure of how to move surely in this place.

Esme turned around and retraced her path home, pedaling hard the whole way. This creature, this spirit, was entirely new to her, and so sweet.

"You're back soon!" Molly exclaimed when she came in the door. "What's up?"

She put her bag on the bench in the mud room slowly. "Oh, nothing. I got a cramp. I'll be all right. Can the delivery wait until next weekend, Mom?"

"Of course. No problem," Molly answered. There was no hurry. The weather was steady and mild this time of year, and her customers knew her deliveries would come when it was convenient for her.

Later that week, however, a freak storm came through. It rained and rained. Roads were flooded out. Creeks overflowed. Basements got four inches of water for the first time in decades. This of course kept the UFOlogists from their "site visit." Most of them had full time jobs in any case, and couldn't jump on traveling to a sighting as soon as they wished.

Raymond Sharpshrifter was surprised by another phone call, this time from the police: there had been a massive mud slide. Right near Oso. The face of an entire ridge--the ridge of "alien doom"--slid down like a dropped souffle, burying houses, part of a highway, and many precious people under it. He wrote, tearfully,

"Disaster in Oso

Up to 70 feet of mud swallowed part of the Stillaguamish River, a mile-long stretch of state highway 530, and 49 homes. Forty-three people lost their lives. The mud tsunami is one of the deadliest in U.S. history. Although many said it was completely unforeseen, recent studies of the hillside warned of the risk which did not result in remedial action. Survivors and victims feel that the State oversight and a timber company that logged extensively on the hillside are culpable."

Mrs. Taylor's little house was spared. It took days to clear the mud that blocked the road to her home. That day, she'd gotten a call to visit her sister in Sedro Woolley. It turned out to be some pseudo-emergency, much to her ire in the moment, except it turned out to save her being cut off from "civilization," unprepared for the ordeal. She felt luckier than others nearby, but now her house was next door to a disaster area, and the neighborhood traumatized, for a long time to come.

Esme told Simon about the mysterious lady in the forest. "Remember, Simon, Caroline told us that some UFO's are controlled mentally by Pleiadians. They're watching over the Earth, and us."

These freakish events made people nervous, of course. Crazy stuff. Work of the devil.

Fire

THE FAMILY WAS JOLTED AWAKE in near darkness by the sound of a crashing noise. Pip flew off of Esme's bed, down the hall, down the stairs, and burst into his most fierce barking. All four of them ran into each other trying to jump down the stairs to the front door at the same time, all of them in sleep clothes: t-shirts, underwear.

"Kids, wait, let me go ahead of you!" shouted Donald.

They could smell smoke. The front of the house was a rustic screened porch with a tin roof.

Donald raced into the porch which was crowded with wooden tables for gardening, and tools like rakes and shovels. A few wicker chairs were set on one side, for sitting and looking out on the woods. The front door was on fire, and the fire blocked their exit. The whole porch was open to air on three sides and ideal for air currents fanning the flames.

"Stay back! Stay back!" he yelled, grabbing a few buckets from the space away from the flames. He backed into the house heading for the kitchen sink. "Molly, go out and try to get to the hose. Try to get to the hose!"

Molly ran out a back door, barefoot, and raced to the side of the house to the outdoor faucet and hose. It was near the outside of the porch but also near flames that had reached the frame of the porch.

Esme stayed with Donald, filling the second bucket as he ran with the first one back into the porch.

Simon ran out with Molly and started pulling the hose from its reel.

She got the water turned on and dragged the nozzle to the front of the house.

The porch had a tin roof. Under it the wooden frame on the entire front was already burned. Some wood stacked against the side was burning like an outdoor bonfire.

Esme hauled the second bucket to pass it to Donald. He handed her the empty one. He was dowsing the wicker chairs that were perfect kindling.

Suddenly the tin roof came crashing down on his head, forcing him into the corner with the wicker. Esme was cut off, holding an empty bucket. Through the door, she could see her mother now on the other side of the fire.

"Moooommm!" she screamed. "Moooommmm!"

The door to the house was bare to open air now, with the tin roof bent down to the ground in front of her. With her father under it. She grabbed the edge of the roof and recoiled with burned hands.

Molly could see the front of the tin roof starting to move down as the wooden braces under it broke into ash. She managed to put out the burning on the outside.

Simon came running on Esme's screams. He ran around to the far side of the porch. By now the tin was buckling and bending down even further. It had disconnected from the siding of the house, now it rested like a giant lid over a cauldron in which Donald was getting cooked.

Esme watched Simon put his hands on the rim of the roof that was barely in his reach, and push. The whole roof moved a few feet away from him. He pushed again, and it slid as if on skids, more than five feet. Then he ducked under it, into smoke, steam, smoldering objects. She saw him pulling his Dad, carefully, slowly, out of the cauldron. He pulled until they were ten feet away, on grass.

Molly couldn't see to that side; she was looking at the fire on her side of the porch: finally dowsed, rising smoke and ash.

Esme ran through the house to the back door, out and around to her Mom.

They could hear sirens, and within minutes neighbors and fire engines were crowding the front yard next to a giant wood stack that fronted them to the street.

"My husband! In back! Please get him! Please!" Molly screamed, pointing to the other side of the tin roof, now nearly flat, surrounded by several feet of burnt structures.

Esme caught up to her and wrapped her arms around her. Two neighbors arrived and wrapped them in blankets. It was an early fall night and fairly warm, but the family were all wearing the equivalent of underwear.

Esme and Molly and the two ladies hugging them walked to where they could see the activity behind the now-scorched remains of their porch.

Several firemen were kneeling around Simon and Donald. Donald was flat on his back. His t-shirt was mostly burnt away. Simon was on his knees leaning over, with two hands on Don's chest. It was not the position for CPR which is what puzzled the onlookers. That would have been on one side or the other, with his hands on top of each other where his heart was. And Simon was not pumping his Dad's heart. He was simply resting hands and humming. One of the firemen held the others back, instinctively understanding that the posture meant something. Finally, Simon picked up his hands and sat back. He looked up as if to signal he was done.

The firemen checked Donald and immediately put a respirator on him. Donald coughed a few times and opened his eyes. There was a collective, "Oh thank God!"

The medics checked his body for burns, checked his bones, his abdomen, his heart. They insisted on taking him to the emergency room but he sat up and declined.

Two others checked Simon. His hands were black with ash but not burned. He was also offered a respirator but declined.

When all had cleared, everyone there could see a burnt cross on the lawn. About four feet tall, burnt but still intact. And next to it, on the grass, were the numbers "6 6 6" in white paint- - the sign of the devil. The firemen immediately pushed people away from the display. They tried to turn the family away from it, now that they weren't literally being consumed by a fire, but they all saw it.

The next day, Raymond Sharpshrifter published an opinion piece in *The Sedro Sentinel:*

"THIS IS NOT US

The fire at the Jensen's last night was a horrible sight to behold. The police are investigating it as a case of arson. Clearly, it was also a crime of hate. We are all shocked that anyone in our community would do such a heinous deed. The family survived the fire without terrible injury. Everyone is in awe of the brave--and seeming miraculous--actions of little ten-year-old Simon. He single-handedly pushed the red-hot tin roof off his trapped father, and pulled him away from the wreckage.

The City Council is offering a reward of $50,000 for tips that lead to the perpetrators. None of us wants to live in a place that repeats atrocities familiar to Americans, from history not that long ago. We all recognize that the fight for civil rights, and civility, is not over, and we hope that everyone will be vigilant in guarding the safety of each and every citizen and friend in Sedro Woolley."

Many families even from Roslyn Millhouse's church brought casseroles and food staples to comfort the Jensens. In a few weeks, a number of pick-up trucks pulled up, and a swarm of strong men rebuilt the front patio and put a new tin roof over it. The local hardware store donated all the materials, including an ironwork patio set to replace the old wicker chairs.

"It feels like all of Sedro Woolley is in our house," Donald mumbled over his first coffee, soon after the fire.

"It must be strange to have people working on your own house," Molly said, "After all those years of picking up junk to patch our house in Oregon. When did you last see brand new boards, and a brand new tin roof, and a nice patio set? When did you last see kind neighbors going out of their way to help us?"

"I'd give it up for some peace of mind," said Donald. "We still don't know who did it."

"Will they do it again?" asked Esme. She was eating a donut from a box donated the day before, still fresh.

"They better not," said Donald. "I'm going to get a gun."

"Don!" Molly jumped around from the stove, cooking eggs. "You can't be serious!"

"You think the police are going to find the culprit and 'bring him to justice.' Hah!"

"Dad, a gunshot sure stopped those boys at the Bug House. Just sayin'," said Esme, looking at Simon.

"That's crazy," said Molly waving her spatula, "You want somebody to get killed. Escalate, get a war going."

"They just nearly killed me," said Donald. "Better them than me."

"They were not trying to kill you, or us," she said, "They wanted to scare us. The house caught on fire from the burning cross. They could have fire-bombed the house directly if they wanted to kill you."

"I want to scare them back, Molly. That's all." He sipped his coffee with both hands.

"The police are watching out for us now. You saw the response. People care about us. You're letting some freaks drive us to a form of madness."

156

"Freaks everywhere. Who's the freaks, Molly?" He stared at her.

Molly pitched her spatula into the sink. "Hey! Hey! You don't say that about your own son!" She went over and hugged Simon from behind and kissed his head, her eyes tearing up. "Oh my God."

Esme started to cry. She got up to leave. Molly waved her to sit. "Stop, Esme. We're not leaving it there." She glared at Donald, who leaned back, flushed. "Don, you apologize to us. We are not freaks. Nobody here is a freak. We don't deserve the hate, and the fire, and the harassment. We have to live with people. We can't just pop away into the woods."

"I'm sorry, kids. Molly. I'm sorry," he said. "But I'm still going to shop guns. And everybody in town will know it."

"You think you'll be able to shoot all the bad guys out of existence, Don? Guns attract guns. Guys love a fight. You're playing right into the kind of life they want--dog eat dog. How many of the guys who worked on the patio were friends of yours? Do you think they want to stay friends with a mad dog? An armed mad dog?"

"Who helped us in Oregon, Molly? Who was going to keep them off my back, and yours?"

"We left. We ran. We didn't give anybody a chance to help. It's not the same. We have help here. Lots of help. Our kitchen is full of food thanks to them. Our porch is brand new, thanks to them." She took up a towel and stroked her face to calm down. "Let's think what Saint Caroline would do."

"What would she do?" asked Esme.

"Oh, baby. I think she would go downtown and hug people. Trust them. Trust a social contract that says we'll all stay decent. We'll be our better selves."

"I'm not hugging anybody," said Esme. "Sherman says stay under the radar."

"Sherman?" Molly looked at Donald. Sherman was a dog. 'Sherman says?'

"Sherman?" Donald said, looking from one child to the other.

"Oh, never mind. I made that up." Esme picked up her dishes and got up. Pleiadians were a special kind of strange.

"What kind of gun?" asked Simon.

Two Houses

WHEN MOLLY BROUGHT CARDBOARD BOXES into the house it felt as if someone had died. In fact, someone had died. Caroline. And they were going to pack up and move into her house.

Molly had waited until Donald was out of the house to start the process, so he wouldn't have to watch. "You don't have to pack everything, kids. You're going to spend time here too. Just, like, half your stuff. Things you want to start out in the new house. It's not like totally leaving one place and having to empty it out."

"Are Caroline's things still there?" asked Esme, thinking about all the trouble they went to, to break into the shed.

"Some. Her sister took a sweep through the house, so you can expect that anything of value is gone. I've been there to move many smaller things into a storage locker. We can make it our own, slowly."

"Mom, what about my favorite pillow? Where does it go?" asked Simon.

"You have to decide, baby. You can also carry it back and forth. Perfectly fine. We want you to feel good in both places." She hugged him.

"Where will Pip, and Penelope, and Persephone live?" Esme crossed her arms and looked around at their pets. Pip-the-schnoodle was upside down, legs in the air, in a favorite dog

159

bed. Black cat Penelope had draped herself the full length of the couch. Persephone-the-Russian-Blue sat pensive, in the doorway to the kitchen.

Yeah, where? Said Pip, to the kids. He didn't change his position, though, apparently unconcerned.

"I'm afraid they'll have to settle into the place they choose," said Molly. "Pip can go back and forth, if you like. If he likes. The cats know the way between the houses. We'll put food out in both places. Okay?" She looked over at Persephone, who started to lick herself.

We'll find you, kids, Persephone signaled. *I'll put you on my rounds, in any case.* She brushed her face with a paw.

"Can we use Caroline's shed?" asked Esme. "We can meet up there."

"Of course you can. I hear a window was broken out, completely. But nothing was taken. The police put a board up over it. You'll have to clean up the glass."

"Should be easy, with the tape on most of the glass," said Simon.

Esme put a fist to her mouth, behind her mother's back. Simon ducked, realizing his mistake.

"What? What tape?" Molly looked at him.

"Oh no. No tape," he said. "Maybe some tape that Caroline used to fix it up. I think."

"We'll clean it up, Mom. Don't worry," said Esme. "Speaking of tape, where's the tape for these boxes?"

Caroline's house had two bedrooms upstairs, and a downstairs study.

When they were alone, Esme whispered to Simon, "Do you think Glyph is going to find you?"

"Oh sure. Anywhere. It's like I have a chip, like a pet. Not really, though. They just don't have any trouble with tracking, is all," he said. "But maybe I'll take the study downstairs so Mom doesn't hear anything."

They moved a mattress from the shed to an upstairs room for Esme, and let Simon have the guest bed in the study.

Donald had been increasingly short with them. The burning cross, the arson of their home, incidents at school, snarky comments from near-strangers about Caroline--all made him feel like an outsider again. An outsider who possibly needed to stay on the run, maybe. He'd fled Portland for a commune. A commune, where Molly and his spirits devolved from euphoria to distress, poverty, disillusion with the dream of a harmonious, prosperous small communal utopia. He'd avoided the decadence of other hippies who fried their brains with drugs and became dissipated, irresponsible. He and Molly had finally gotten on their feet financially. The kids were healthy. The kids were in school. They hadn't conformed to tradition in every way: they'd given up on a commune but they hadn't given up on "their own way." They weren't married. They were free spirits in a tight bond, on a common mission to live their own lives the way they wanted. Now some kind of occult thing landed in their private utopia. It was yet a new threat that seemed beyond his control, or even his understanding, this time.

"I can't lose the job, Molly," he said. "I can't support us without the job. There aren't that many jobs to be had. And if they think we're freaks, then we're done here."

"I know, I know."

The biggest rift was over Simon's "situation." Donald couldn't buy into the "ET theory" about Simon. He wanted to

161

follow the medical advice to medicate, and limit the experiences Simon had, that seemed symptoms of psychosis or hallucinations. Molly only saw the urge to "put him in the Bug House" and classify something that was surely not ordinary, but surely not mental illness. The word "aliens" had not figured into the disorders that sent people to the Bug House. She wanted Simon to keep control over his "treatments" whatever they may be.

They sat the kids down for a frank talk.

"Simon," Donald said to his little son, "Are you sure these aren't nightmares? Fantasies?"

"No," said Simon. "I'm sure. They're good for me. I'm fine."

"He's like in super-hero training, Dad," added Esme. "It's like Star Trek, only for real." She had heard Simon talk about his experiences from age five onward, and he never sounded like he was scared, or messed up. In fact, he slept soundly, and he was acting with such wisdom that she might even feel jealous.

"We can't encourage this, Simon," Donald said to him and looked at Molly and Esme. "You've got to pull back. Can you do that?"

"It's not up to me, Dad," said Simon. "Not up to me. There's some kind of pace to it, but I don't know what it is. Doesn't bother me."

"You mean it's out of control?" Donald said sharply. "Your life, and mine, and our family life, is in the hands of aliens?"

"Not aliens, Dad," said Simon. "Glyph, my guide. He's like a master guardian. He won't let anything happen to me."

"Like boys killing you in an abandoned building?"

"They didn't kill him, in fact," said Esme, quietly.

"Oh stop, Esme. You're both too young to realize what people are capable of doing to you! You're not living with aliens,

162

and whatever their rules. You're living in Sedro Woolley, and some people don't like us. The way we are." He got up and paced the kitchen.

"Donald, we're not the only strange people in Sedro Woolley. They'll forget some of this stuff, soon enough."

"Molly," he slapped his hand on the kitchen counter, "Do I need to remind you that I nearly got killed in Oregon?"

"Huh?" said Simon.

"Mom?" said Esme.

"Wait. Donald. Aliens. White supremacists. Racists. Religious fanatics. Where can we run to? What do you suggest?" Molly stood up. "Maybe a cave?"

"No, no. Not a cave. How about we hide a little. Lay low. I've got to keep the job. I've just GOT to keep the job." His face flushed.

"I know you like the job. And we need it. We need you to function." Molly touched his shoulder. "How about the kids and I move into Caroline's house and you stay here. Calm down."

"You mean quit each other? Are you serious?" He teared up. The kids teared up. Everybody looked at everybody else in shock.

"No, no, Donald. We lower the temperature a bit. Do you know that you've gotten belligerent? Crabby? You're snapping at everyone. That's not going to keep the job."

"Right."

"We've got two houses. We'll take some time to sort out Simon's thing," she smiled at Simon, "and you get away from being upset about it every day. We get stronger by calming down. Don't let other people think we've gone over some edge and they need to make it their business, or push us further away."

"Right."

"Short-term, Donald. You keep going to work. You calm down. You act like the strong steady man you are. We don't break, in public. We divide, and conquer these bad vibes." Molly moved next to him and put her arm around him.

"Sounds like an excuse to get rid of me." He returned her hug.

"It's a way to keep you, Donald. And remember, we own Caroline's house now. We can sell a house if things get really bad. We have more resources than ever."

"Okay," he looked at Simon and Esme. "Okay?"

They were frozen, sitting at the dining table. The green jello with whipped cream in their bowls quivered. It was forgotten.

It was awful to live as nomads. Esme woke up in the morning and tried to remember where she was, and where was the bathroom, even the light switch on the wall. Whether she had school clothes for today in this place. The light and dark patterns inside the house, in the course of the day. Where were the dark corners, where did you need to turn on a light? Where were the cats today? Would they see them?

They could walk to school from either house but the distance was different, so it took a different amount of time to get to school.

Every automatic decision of rushed mornings was crowded with concentration. It couldn't be automatic.

Pip tried to keep up and sometimes just chose to stay in one place rather than switch mid-week.

Sometimes they had plenty of milk and cereal in one place but the place they woke up the next morning had no milk and cereal.

164

They didn't complain because Donald was on edge and Molly would hover over them for days, feeling guilty.

They tried to have family dinners on Friday nights at Caroline's house, so Molly could cook, but if Donald was between shifts, he was exhausted and just wanted to have a beer and stare into space.

"When do we stop this, Molly?" he asked. "What's the end game? Are we separating forever?"

"No, Donald. We're trying to get through a few months without incident. We all want to forget the turbulence. Let the town forget we exist."

"Well, Simon," Donald turned to his son. "Are things quiet on your front?"

Esme piped in. "Dad, he's never acted like anything was wrong. It's the other people!"

"Dad, I'm okay. Really," said Simon. "Please don't blame me. I didn't do anything."

"I know, Simon," Donald said, "I just want to know about the other creatures in our lives. What they're up to."

"They're good. They're good for me, Dad." Simon crossed his arms on his chest.

"Who's the enemy here, Donald," asked Molly. "I think it's your fear of the town. They're obsessed with Caroline and her stuff. Not us. We don't have to act like this is all about us."

"Molly, blue marks. All over his body. The town knows about that."

"Why won't people just leave us alone, Mom?" asked Simon. "We haven't hurt anybody, have we?"

"I think it's about being 'the wrong kind,' Simon," said Donald. "They have some idea that we're a threat to their way of life. Whether it's true or not."

165

Molly stepped in. "But this is America, kids. It's Sedro Woolley. There are lots of different folks here, and there are laws against aggressions and violence. We have to just fade out of their vision. Let them get over Caroline. We have to hope other things get more important than harassing us about our beliefs, or our life style."

"When, Mom? When?" Esme teared up. "I don't want to fight. I don't want to hide." Sometimes she lost her perspective, that this reality was one of many, with a unique set of tribulations, and that everybody including Pleiadians, would incarnate many times, every life a fiction of a sort. The human child in her Earthly body had simple emotions, too.

"I know, baby. Let's just go on for a bit, and take it a day at a time. Can you do that, kids?" she asked, but pointedly looked at Donald.

Glyph Visits

THE PATTERN OF NIGHT LIGHTS was different in the study in Caroline's house, where Simon slept. As the sun set, the corner where his treasured Star Trek things clustered would first light up and then go dark. His Spiderman poster dominated the room and then went black unless he switched on a light. His Leggos were spread on a desk and turned from a cacophony of color into a black sculpture made of black, sharp-edged hoodoos.

When they moved into Caroline's house, he and Esme decided he would take the first-floor room and she would sleep upstairs. They thought that he would be more accessible to Glyph and the others, and far from Molly who also slept upstairs. The room faced the back yard--the very same back yard in which Caroline's shed stood, its back window still broken.

In the middle of the night, Simon opened his eyes, for no reason at all. He knew there was a reason, though. A vapor, like a mist, but not thick like smoke, appeared against the wall opposite the window, which he kept uncovered. On clear, moonlit nights, his room was full of a magic glow as if he were outside in the woods or on a beach. With seconds the shape of Glyph morphed out of the vapor. Simon was delighted to see him because he was like a funny friend: the long arms and legs, the bird's foot hand with a thumb and three fingers. Glyph was short and looked vulnerable, like a child.

167

"Hi," Simon said sleepily, turning toward the vapor.

Glyph raised his "claw" to the place where his mouth might be, if he had one. He looked like a cartoon with the bulbous head and pointy ears, a thatch of light hair sticking straight up.

As Simon got up, three others appeared out of the vapor, wearing shiny dark-blue, form-fitting uniforms with little emblems on their sleeves. Unlike Glyph, they wore gloves and high boots. They got into their "travel" formation, a line with Glyph in front and Simon sandwiched among the three companions. In a swooping motion, he was no longer walking, but floating several inches above the ground. His body felt weightless.

The five entities passed through the wall, through solid wood, to the back yard. Instantaneously, it seemed to Simon, they were in the space ship. He knew now that they had ways-- converters?-- to break down the matter of the body into fine-matter or energy, and them reassemble it inside the ship. It caused no special sensation in him--the only way he knew it had happened was that his mind recognized the new place.

Glyph engulfed Simon in a physical hug of love that gave him the sensation of the most extraordinary good feeling he'd ever felt. It was a reward for their friendship, for his acceptance of his contract with the aliens, for being part of the team.

Are you getting sensations from the implant in your brain, Simon? Especially when you're falling asleep? asked Glyph.

"Yes, I am. I hear faint sounds. I feel something like a vibration in my body," he answered.

Then it's working. We're using that to transmit information to you all the time. You're like a receiver for a radio station. Glyph laughed. He'd learned enough about humans to "speak their language." *It also blocks signals that may be directed at you to foil ours, or that may try to control your mind.*

"Wow. Is anybody trying to do that?" Simon asked.

Not yet. Glyph raised his hand as if in a "hallelujah" gesture. *The implants also enhance the defenses of your own brain, including your unconscious. Like magnifiers of your defensive instincts.*

"Cool." Simon's long experience with Star Trek and such gave him an appreciation for any super powers or enhancers to everyday human powers.

It's also awakening your DNA to your awareness of your existence in the system of the universe. Most humans are sleep-walking, by comparison.

"Ahh." Simon pictured the zombie movies he'd seen. "But what about Esme? Is she being awakened too?"

Esme is a different energy construct than you, Simon. She is developing on her own without our implants. Her DNA was already activated when she was born.

This was puzzling to Simon. As long as she's not sleep-walking, he thought. We want to be together in our powers, he thought, not too different.

Let's go to the lab and try some new things, Glyph said, turning toward a door.

They were moving through a room that looked like an operating arena. There were bright lights shining into the room from sources he didn't recognize. They were not lamps. The walls were lined with large gray devices on all sides in shapes he didn't recognize. About a dozen creatures were gathered around a metallic platform.

As they passed closely around the backs of the circled creatures, Simon glanced over at the platform. There was the shape of a human! A fully clothed human! A woman! Who appeared to be asleep, on her back! As they moved by, he got a better look at her face.

ROSLYN MILLHOUSE.

It was all he could do to swallow the "WHAT!!??" in his throat. He only knew her from passing in the streets in town, but she'd been pointed out as the lady who's said bad things about Caroline. Man, he thought, Esme's not going to believe this.

There was a big purple light over her face, pulsating, like a heartbeat. Outside the purple light was a green glow, with an indigo, iridescent rim. The purple light projected shapes, patterns like snowflakes, six-sided figures, spirals, triangles, over her body.

Glyph could tell he recognized her, but pulled Simon past as they were going to another room.

When they got to the other room, Simon was beside himself. "Glyph, what are they doing? Are they hurting her? Are they implanting?"

No, no, Simon. We've been studying her for a long time. She doesn't know it.

"You mean she doesn't talk to you like I do?"

No. We visit her from time to time. Harmless. No implants. No marks left behind. She doesn't know it. She might one day realize she has 'missing time' like other abductees, but we've avoided letting her be aware.

"You mean, she isn't scared?"

We erase her memory. We don't want her to feel fear or anything else. No impact. That's the category she's in. You see?

"Yeah. I guess. You know she's a very religious lady, right? She'd probably die on the spot if she knew about this."

She won't know. Her belief system doesn't matter to us. We're all energy, Simon, right? Basically, the same, give or take certain dimensions of reality. Glyph laughed.

Skagit River Flood

THE ANNUAL SKAGIT VALLEY SALMON FESTIVAL was a big party in September. There was a beer and wine garden, art, crafts, food stations, and live music. Esme went with her mother to set up a special farmer's market booth to sell mums in fall colors, decorative squash, and corn. A gigantic statue of a salmon attracted a swarm of kids climbing and crawling inside. It celebrated the unique place of fish in the lives along the Skagit River: it was the largest river system in Washington state that contained healthy populations of all five native salmon species (chinook, coho, chum, pink, sockeye) and two trout (steelhead and coastal cutthroat.) The river was a major spawning habitat, so its waters were packed with fish on a mission.

The Cabal welcomed the return of other migrating creatures, too, some related to the fish. The valley had one of the largest populations of bald eagles, 600 to 800, returned for the winter and the feast of salmon. They came from Canada, Alaska, and Montana. The assembly of eagles was joined by the dramatic return of snow geese, who fed on the marsh plants and potatoes left in the fields after harvest. Another vision of migration were the several hundred trumpeter swans. Among these beautiful animal flocks and gatherings were always a few familiar Pleiadians. Sherman, Pip, the cats and others loitered on the edge of certain fields as a Committee of Welcome. They had their own festivals, catching up on news from around the country.

Esme was busy unloading a truck and a van onto wagons that could reach the farmer's market booth, set among others on the grassy riverside.

"The rains on Mt. Baker aren't doing us any favors," said a neighbor putting crafts on display, speaking to Molly. "Last week was unusually bad, this early in the fall. It's not melting snow, right now. It's simply heavy rain."

"Oh my," Molly said. "Do you think we're in trouble here?"

"Not, here, I think. But up river in Lyman and Hamilton, they get worried. The whole of Hamilton has thought about moving instead of getting wiped out all the time."

"The whole town?"

"All 300 of them. Imagine having to worry every year. They had big evacuations in 2003, and 2006, when water reached four feet right in the middle of town. The city sits in the middle of the flood plain, which wasn't smart, but it worked for a hundred years or so."

Another booth neighbor chimed in, "The water was too high for regular boats to be used in rescue. They had to bring in hovercraft. The RVs there are required to have quick disconnect and be road-ready for emergency evacuation."

"Where do they go?" asked Molly.

"Across the highway, to a church parking lot. Or, anyplace they have friends and family."

There was a radio on, that carried reports of water-level gauges and warnings from County services. People were clustered around an enlarged Flood Warning Map mounted on an upright board that showed areas that were likely to be affected when certain levels were reached in certain places.

While Esme tried to get a good look at the map, another conversation took place at the "local news" booth, where a writer for the *Sentinel* sat.

"What happened with the UFO? Anybody call you up?" asked a burly man, who looked like he was in construction or lumber.

"No, no," said the reporter. "We're still waiting."

"Any UFO chasers show up?"

"Not that we know, Roger," he said. "They didn't give us a call, in any case."

"Them UFOs. Anybody worried about abductions? Or invasion?"

"Not really. We have to have evidence."

"You heard about the kid with the blue marks all over him?
"

"Nobody figured out what that was, Roger. A medical mystery. No harm done. The kid's all right."

"Probably too many movies, huh?"

"Yeah. Invasion of the blue people. *Avatar*. We've got enough on our hands without'em." They both laughed.

A phone call interrupted their chat. "What?!" said the writer, "Give me the facts." He wrote furiously. Then he got on a microphone hooked to a loudspeaker.

"People, attention. Attention. People," he said. "We just got word that some levees up river have given way. There will be more water coming down than we thought. It could take twelve hours for the flood waters to reach us here down river, but don't think that's a guarantee. This is an emergency! I repeat, it's an emergency! We should expect the river to rise up maybe four feet here in Sedro Woolley. If you're on the river, get cracking!"

The festival spirit broke in a second. People got on cell phones, ran to their cars, started gathering up goods on display.

Esme ran back to Molly. "Mom, did you hear?"

Molly nodded. "We need to pack up, quick." They pulled wagons to the tables and started transferring flower pots to them. They were done in thirty minutes. Molly shut the doors on the van and the truck, and got into the van. A friend was coming to drive the second vehicle away.

"Mom, Mom," said Esme. "I want to go check the river. Please."

"You heard the man, Esme. It's rising fast."

"I know. But I'll stay on high ground. Okay?"

"Okay. You come home in an hour or two, okay? Or I'll come after you," she said.

Esme followed a crowd moving quickly away from the festival grounds. They were already riverside, but the road led away. She knew there was a small RV park just a few blocks away, on the river. It was a wonderful patch of real estate, for the view of the hundred-foot-wide river and woody hills on the other side. Most of the banks of the river were wild, rough growth. You could hardly access the river through the growth. This patch of settlement was unusually flat, extending out so at least five RV's were lined up on the banks with shoreside access, with only paths between them for the others to get to the water.

The water had already risen to cover grass on the waterside outcrop, completely. Panicked occupants were carrying boxes and suitcases from their RV to a car parked as near as possible, between the other RVs.

A sudden rush of water rose to two feet deep. Pets were carried up to the higher bank. People watching the scene helped by holding pets and small children. A small playground next to the RV's was now in a lake. Play bridges and ladders were like real refuge platforms. You didn't want to go down the slide-- there was nothing but water at the bottom.

There was almost no activity at one of the RV's. When the water got to four feet, the door opened into the water and a girl leaned out from the outside steps.

"Help!" she called. "Help. My parents are gone. I don't know what to do!"

The gathered gawkers suddenly became witnesses to a crisis beyond rescuing things. The girl had waited much too long.

"Call 911!" somebody yelled. Another pulled out a cell phone and dialed.

The crowd including Esme were standing on a knoll just above the water's edge.

The distance from them to the RV was about a hundred feet. The water was still rising, and starting to flow with currents amidst the RVs. The RV's were now in the middle of river.

As everyone looked around in a panic for a boat, or some means to reach the girl, they focused on an old zip line. There were pylons in the river from the old steamboat days. There had been a canoe ferry from the knoll they were standing on. A zip line was still in place, that crossed the entire river. It happened to pass close to the girl's RV.

"The rope's no good," said Roger, the burly man whom Esme had overheard at the news table earlier. "It won't hold me. It's old."

"Maybe the girl can get to it and pull herself in," said someone.

"She's too upset. We don't know if she's strong enough. The current's picking up. It's too risky."

"It might hold me," said Esme, walking up to Roger. "I think I could get out there." She was remembering the incident long, long ago, when she fell off a tree trunk and Caroline rescued her. Since then, she'd ventured out on many trees and through many rivers.

"Wait for the firemen, I say," said someone else.

"That RV could just pick up and float away, the way things are going."

"I say let her try it. Anybody have a rope we can put on her? Any life jackets?"

Someone ran to their car and got two life jackets from their trunk. They were big, but one was put on Esme and then the extra rope strapped it tight on her.

"Now, girlie," said Roger, who was doing most of the tying, "That zip line could break. We'll have you on a line, like a fish. Your goal is to get the other girl in a jacket and tied to you. Got it?"

"Like a fish. Right."

They tied the other jacket to the rope so that if the other girl was in it, the two of them would both be on the rope. And another loop was on the zip line.

Esme was wearing shorts and a T-shirt. She'd thrown off her hoodie, needed for cooler September weather. She kept her sandals on, because she would be walking through the water. She shouldn't have to swim unless things got much, much worse.

She stepped into the freezing water. The Skagit was not even swimmable in the summer, because the water came off the mountains. Most of the year, it was water that was melted snow and ice. At least it was clean. She moved the loop on the zip line forward and then stepped after it.

"We're coming," yelled Roger to the girl. "Don't let go of the door there. Don't step into the water without a rope on you. We're getting a rope to you."

The girl nodded. She was wet from standing in the water that was mid-way up the stairs into the RV, and she hung onto the door.

Esme felt the current drag her downriver. The river pulled her and the zipline tight. She kept her footing but now had to hold the loop and zipline with both hands to keep her balance.

Finally, she got within feet of the RV.

"Hey," she said, keeping an eye on her hands and the zipline. "Hold on. I'll get to you."

It was the bully Wanda. The girl who'd called her a coon head. The girl she'd said had roaches in her hair. They were made for each other.

Caroline, Esme thought. Caroline, help me out. Please.

Finally, she got to the door, pulling the zipline tight to get there. "You need to get into the jacket, and make it tight. Can you do that?"

"I think so."

"Don't let go of the door. Whatever you do, don't let go. The river's after us both, you hear?" She looked into Wanda's frightened eyes. "We'll be together. But you've got to be careful, for both of us. Hear?"

"Yes." Wanda reached an arm into the jacket, then turned inside it to change arms on the door and get the other arm in. They two of them buckled it, and tightened it as much as possible. They were a pair of orange bobbles now, hanging from a loop on the zip line.

"We're good," she shouted back at Roger.

He saw her wave. "Going to pull, now. You girls hang onto each other and the rope. You might let go of the zipline. It could burn when we pull you. Okay?"

He and two other men slowly pulled the rope, hoping the friction would not break the zipline. Two orange bobbles floated pulling away hard from the zip line, hanging by a loop. If the line broke, they would bobble down the river, but, like fish on a line, they could be pulled in.

It didn't break. When they were just ten feet from the shore, the emergency rescue crew pulled up. A man in waders jumped out. He was just in time to help them stumble out of the water.

The cluster of worried people shouted "Yay!" "Good job!" "Oh my God!"

As they got the girls untethered, unknotted, and unbuckled, Esme said, "I've got to get home. Really."

Wanda whispered, "Thank you. Thank you." She was crying now--there was no need to hold it together any more. They'd almost become fish, almost about to join the others in the river. Rescue people threw blankets on them both.

"Don't you want us to check you out?" they asked Esme.

"No, I'm good. Just went for a swim," she said. Then she pulled away and found her hoodie on the grass. One of the town ladies gave her a ride home.

When she got home, Molly was impatient. "I asked you to come back in a few hours. I was about to climb in the car."

Esme shrugged her shoulders. "We had to help out. The RVs got flooded. People were trapped."

"Wow. That was nice of you." Molly got a towel from the laundry. "And thanks for helping with the mums, too. Why are you completely soaked?"

The Kindness of Strangers

"ESME, SOMEONE FROM SOCIAL SERVICES wants to chat with you briefly," said her teacher. "Is that okay?"

"Why would they want to do that?" Esme looked up from her reading. They were in the midst of quiet time, and she was reading *A Wrinkle In Time*, where Meg goes off looking to find her father, who is missing in a far galaxy. The story seemed too close to home, actually. She got up and closed the book very slowly, like a chore she would not do if her teacher were not standing right over her.

They walked to the counselor's offices which had a small room for private conversations. It was an ugly room with no decoration, not even butterflies and flowers and ocean scenes like a dentist office. The furniture looked like cast-offs from an older version of the school: a small square wooden table and wooden hard-back chairs. Esme had seen rooms like this before, on TV shows that feature police interrogators.

"Why hello, dear," said a voice in the door. A short, stout woman appeared, wearing a suit jacket that was too tight--the kind of suit women will wear who think they need to look "professional" and who then tear the thing off the minute they get home. Her short hair was unflattering, and Esme felt bad for her. If she were a kid in school, she would surely get teased for not having any flare at all.

"Hello," said Esme, quietly.

"I just wanted to touch base with you. A few things have happened recently that would seem to be upsetting, and we want to look out for you." The woman sat down and folded her hands in front of her. "I'm Mrs. Dinsdale," she reached out her hand.

Esme put her elbows on the table and folded her hands under her chin, ignoring the outstretched hand. She tried not to frown.

"How's your little brother doing, after that bullying incident?"

"Fine."

"Is he still being bothered?" Her smile was caring and warm.

"You'll have to ask him."

The smile turned into tense lips. "And how are you? I hear you were quite the hero in getting him away from the boys." She smiled again.

"Fine."

"You were very brave." The lady paused. She took a folder from her large purse and opened it on the table. "Are you still living at ....?"

"Yes."

"And your parents are both there?"

Esme gave her a blank look. The fact that she and her mom had moved into Caroline's house could not have been widely known, but it was a small town. Somebody could have seen them leave from there one morning, and there you are. They had barely had a few breakfasts alone, already, without their Dad, and the kitchen seemed empty of his morning bustle. No one spoke in the mornings, for fear of tearing up, and getting upset right on the way to school for the day.

"You can be frank with me, dear," Mrs. Dinsdale said. "We do all we can to help families through some hard times. Nothing to be ashamed of."

A long silence.

"Are your parents actually married, dear? I heard that they moved up from Oregon and might have been among those people who lived fairly free of social rules. At least for a while." She shuffled her papers, unnecessarily, since there was no reason to pick them up or disturb them. "Don't we all wish there weren't so many rules. Right, dear?" Her smile was now phony, like gesture learned and practiced in social services training: how to *seem* nice.

Esme closed her eyes. She sent thoughts to her mother: come, come and get me. She sent thoughts to Caroline-in-spirit: help me get out of here. Please Caroline, please come in. I don't know what to do. Esme imagined herself in an aura of white light, the protection Caroline had taught her that she now could call up very easily. Her body relaxed in the white light, as if it had disappeared from the immediate scene.

"Of course, we could research this, but I wondered if you knew," the lady said.

Esme opened her eyes slowly. She looked over the lady so awkward in her body and clothes--stuffed into conforming to an uncomfortable dress code, afraid to reject it, afraid to be at ease; afraid to feel pretty, afraid to feel warm? Esme felt the gentle touch of Caroline's spirit come through in her bubble of white light. "Why yes, Mrs. Dinsdale," she said, looking straight into the lady's eyes for a change. "My father is from the ancient Oomadakus in Africa. In fact, he is royalty, so there are rather elaborate rituals involved. The marriage itself takes twenty days of special activities and meals. It takes that long to call up 20

183

years of ancestors, who have to approve the bond. So they are quite married. I'm sure."

Florence Dinsdale sat back, as if large wild and exotic animal had just appeared behind Esme. "Oh, my."

"Are you married, Mrs. Dinsdale?" asked Esme. "Because if you didn't marry in the Oomadaku way, then you're a sinner." Esme tried to imitate the face of a Baptist preacher when he looked into the congregation after a long tirade about purity. She didn't have a lot of experience with Baptist preachers, except for fragments of scenes on TV, and the one week of summer Bible school she'd attended. It was probably a cliché, but she enjoyed putting on the mask.

"I am indeed, Esme." She straightened up. "But let's get back to you and your family. Wasn't your little brother covered in bruises? Bruises that could not be explained?"

"Well, he has darker skin. You could say he's bruised all over, all the time. Right?"

She gasped.

As it happened, the principal, Mr. Bright, pushed the open door further open, and leaned in. "Everything all right in here, Florence? I heard you stopped by."

She straightened up and flushed. "Why of course, Charles. Just fine." She looked anxiously over at Esme.

Esme moved her clasped hands down from her chin. She still had them clasped, in front of her. She looked up at Mr. Bright, frankly appealing to him. "Mr. Bright, I don't feel safe here," she said.

"What?" He pulled the rest of his body into the room. He looked at Esme bewildered. Then at Florence. "What's going on?"

"I want my mom," said Esme. "I don't feel safe. I really need my mom." She put her palms up against her mouth as if stifling a sob. "I want to go home."

He moved to stand right up against the table between them, as if forming a barrier between the two. "Florence, we're going to have to leave it at that," he said, leaning over the table in the direction of Florence Dinsdale. "Esme, you're excused. You can go home if you like. I'll walk you out."

Esme got up, bumping the chair behind her as if rushing to get away. She nearly jumped out of the room.

"Florence. Later," said the principal over his shoulder, rushing out after Esme.

He tried to catch up running down the long hallway. "Are you all right? What happened?"

She avoided his friendly reach for her shoulder. "I can't talk about it, Mr. Bright. I can find my way home, thanks." She ran for the exit.

Pyramid

AFTER FAILING TO GET ANY CLUES from the ghosts at the Bug House, the Cabal kept looking for The Find. They took a long walk to Farmer John's place.

He was in the creek behind his main property, knee-deep in water, the cold clear river stream bathing his bare feet. He leaned over moving rocks in the creek bed, because his house depended on the flow for water.

The Cabal lined up, like a search party, on a small wooden bridge across the creek, about five feet above his head. Carl-Crow was on a branch overhead, preferring his superior vantage point.

John laughed when he saw them. "What's this?" His wet hands rested on his hips. "Are you all going to jump in?"

No, said Pip. *Water? Are you kidding?* Schnoodles didn't like water.

"We're here on business, Mr. John," said Simon.

"Business? Are you going to do some work for me?" he laughed again.

"Well, not this time," said Esme. "We're looking for a lunch box that disappeared."

"Lunch box?"

"Caroline's lunch box. We got it out of her shed and stashed it in a tree, and it disappeared."

"Really?" He knew about Caroline's death, of course. He'd been one of her regular customers, a friend, and a handyman for her.

"It's got Hindu gods on it."

"Not seen it. I'm sorry. Sounds important." He was gentle, as always, towards them.

"All right," said Esme. "We've gotta keep looking." She hadn't expected to get an answer but felt they had to make the effort. "Can we ask you something else?" she said, as she sat down on the edge of the bridge, letting her feet dangle down. Simon copied her move. The four-legged members let their haunches down. Story time?

"What happened to Caroline? How'd she just disappear?" Esme asked.

John wiped his face with his wet hands, and ran them through his straggling hair. A few streaks of mud were created on his cheeks but he couldn't see them. They looked painted on, like a shaman's decoration just before a ritual.

"You know I was close to Caroline, like you," he said.

They nodded.

"Let me tell you the long story. When Caroline was nineteen and upset that her parents couldn't afford to send her to college, she worked in a coffee shop in Bellingham. She lived at home but avoided her parents and managed to be fairly independent.

"One day a boy attending Western Washington University came in and saw a beautiful girl with exotic eyes and thick, long brown hair in the job of barista. You know, you can imagine Caroline at nineteen.

"It turned out that he was studying anthropology in graduate school and was about to travel to India for field work. Most of the university is undergraduate, but he was older. In one of the international studies institutes. He'd managed to get a grant to do field work. He invited her to come to West Bengal with him. He had enough money to support both of them there.

"A side trip to an ashram in Assam changed her life. She discovered Buddhism and spent most of her time reading and visiting a society in Calcutta while the boy did his research in villages an hour away.

"When it came time to return to the States, she decided to stay. An ashram had invited her to stay as a volunteer and they arranged for a long-term visa. She and the boy had cooled on each other by then. They were both young and drunk with life, but no longer on the same path. He wanted to become a professor. She wanted to become a practicing Buddhist.

"She ended up in an ashram on the outskirts of Dharamsala, the home-in-exile of the Dalai Lama and the home-in-exile of Tibetan refugees and Western people who'd discovered them, or who wanted to help sustain them.

"The Western people there dabbled in religious rituals, took meditation courses, and devoted many hours every day working in kitchens, teaching English or other languages, and helping run a refugee settlement.

"Caroline learned about Western women who had become serious Buddhists. Historically, her idol, Alexandra David-Neel. And some contemporaries like the American Pema Chodron who ran an abbey in Nova Scotia, and the English Tenzin Palmo who founded a convent located just hours away from Dharamsala. Tenzin was famous for her twelve-year total seclusion in a cave in the Himalayas, at 13,000 feet elevation.

"With support from the ashram, Caroline was set up in a remote cave. It had all the basics she needed. Perched like an eagle on the top of the world, she was isolated from the noise and clutter of daily life.

"She told me, 'I loved the absolute silence. It was a depth of silence in which the voice of the Absolute could be heard. No interruptions.' She saw no one for several years.

"You know her last name, Milarep?"

"Yes," said Esme. They all nodded.

"She'd read a famous biography of a saint called Milarepa, by Evan-Wentz. Milarepa was one of Tibet's most beloved poet-saints, and famous for meditating in a cave. Eleventh Century. He practiced black magic. He had a staff, a cloak, a bowl, and nothing else. He disappeared into the high mountains, where, in freezing cold and with nothing to eat but nettles, his body became skeletal and his flesh turned entirely green. But he learned to raise his body heat through ecstasy. It's a mystic heat. He could also travel at great speeds. Farmers saw him flying across the valleys.

"It was said that lamas could 'fly', could materialize and dematerialize things at will, they could turn themselves into animals or whatever form them wished, they could travel improbable distances in next to no time by a strange trance-like jumping method.

"One of the things they could do is disintegrate. Do you understand what I'm saying?"

"Sort of."

"They 'dissolve' into pure energy. Disappear. They basically burn up without fire. Can you imagine?"

"That's what Caroline did?"

"I think so."

"But why," asked Simon. "Why did she leave us if she didn't have to?"

Esme started to tear up, staring down at the river. It felt as if Caroline had just left them all over again. Just when Esme was starting to understand the world according to Caroline.

The Cabal was silent. The soothing sound of the river filled the air. John unexpectedly shifted his feet to new positions, leaned down, and picked up a rock the size of a grapefruit. He stood up, and tossed it to a new place, making a big splash.

"Guys," said John, as he turned back to them. "Try the pyramid. Go on." He knew they had to learn some things through their own direct experience.

They understood.

The cabal crossed a large field of tall grass to the edge of the forest. No one was mowing this grass. It was feed for lamas and horses on Farmer John's forty acres.

Farmer John was often busy sawing tree trunks and splitting wood for his house, which was heated by a wood furnace in the basement, sending hot air up a shoot through the center of the house. The heating system was quite old-fashioned. So last century. And a delight. Real fire, making burning, semi-controlled heat, flowing up and out into living spaces. It required the 'honest' labor of chopping down trees, sawing them (a modern method), and then using a wood-splitter to make firewood (also modern). Real, sweet wood-fired heat and its smell permeating your cozy little rooms. Reaching to your down-covered simple bed, and flushing your weathered face.

Farmer John was also like the Alaska off-the-grid folks, downing trees and turning them magically into boards that would be used to build living quarters as walls, shelves, ramps, out-houses. John liked to create his world with his hands. No Home Depot stuff. He knew where his wood came from. He was also blessed in having wood and land to harvest. He never forgot--every shed he built was inaugurated with a prayer. Like Native Americans, he thanked the Earth for its bounty, and he thanked himself, thus The Source, for having the sense to co-create a world, rather than feed off the labor of under-paid economic slaves.

Around Lake Whatcom, not far from John, rich people's mini-mansions had taken up every square foot of lake-shore property. Lavish eight-bedroom, multi-story mini-Alpine villas cropped up, with sloping greens to the waterfront, a generous dock reaching far into the lake, speed boats, boat houses, cabanas for changing clothes and storing the most advanced gear, and caterer's quarters clustered like the estates of a modern nobility. Some properties were fenced to make it clear who was allowed "in" and who was to be kept "out."

Meanwhile, John was the blessed master of his domain. Also, he had a secret domain (the network of vortex sheds), and secret admirers, in the cabal. Who loved him for his very existence in their world.

The cabal reached a pocket of space nestled against the woods, wherein stood a giant wooden pyramid. It was square, about 15 feet on a side, and 15 feet high. Those challenged by geometry might quibble. Since ancient times, as humans knew them (e.g., the Great Pyramid of Giza), and ancient times as aliens knew them (e.g. Atlantis), the pyramid was an energy machine. Disney World for the cabal. They gathered around it: seven of them. They were giddy even without the energy boost inside the pyramid. It was anticipation. Collective anticipation and energy.

"Please," said Esme. "Caroline, we miss you. Please."

They all pictured Caroline. To picture was to realize. Or at least to help to realize.

Yo Caroline, said Sherman. *Please come in.*

They waited patiently. It was an overcast afternoon. The grasses they'd crossed were damp but not a swamp.

It had been months since Caroline disappeared. It seemed like eons to Esme and Simon, with all the drama at home. They felt battle-weary. Leaderless. Sherman and Esme had held things together, but there was missing the familiar posture of dependence on a creature stronger than yourself that you trusted. Someone whose bosom was inviting your rest. A favorite face, a favorite encouraging smile. Someone who seemed to promise that evil forces would not reach you. An angel, really.

Inside the pyramid, the air was stirring. What seemed like humidity was forming a cloud, or a mist, or a ghost. It's shape was nebulous at first, like an amoeba trying to get comfortable hanging in the air. Then a few features of Caroline came clear: her height, a strong light where her heart might have been, then her ample cloak of gray hair, and then her face.

Ooooo, said Pip, the most optimistic among them.

Aaaaaaah, said a cat, normally a skeptical and oblivious cat. You would think a favorite gathering of birds had just landed on a branch nearby.

Caw Caw Caw said Carl, as if a feast of uncovered morsels had landed in a patch of grass shielded from interrupting intruders.

"Huh," gasped Esme. She took a deep breath to keep from fainting.

"Hi! Hi!" exclaimed Simon, jumping in place. His body had to release the tension.

"My dears," said the vision of Caroline. "Please don't try to touch me. Fragile."

"No. Of course not," said Esme as if she knew.

"Fifth dimension thing," said vision-of-Caroline. "Pops in a second."

They stared at each other. Like Jesus risen from the dead, a miracle. Only it was good old Caroline. So sweet.

"I can't stay long," said vision-of-Caroline. "Here: Be strong. You're not alone. You have a mission--to raise vibrations, help others rise above negativity. Don't worry about what they say."

They collectively sighed. It was like finding Mom after some horrible experience. The bosom of Mom.

"What's the lesson of life? To do something. To make the most of whatever happens. It's up to you to be what you're going to be. You might feel defeated, and want to step away. It's worse if you don't try." She smiled. Like an angel. The wood beams in a square around her rose to a point above, seeming to work to boost her into tenuous focus. "I am with you all the time, dears. Do you know that?"

Yes, nodded Pip.

Of course, said Sherman.

Esme burst into tears.

"We're good," said Simon. "Thanks." He'd taken over speaking for Esme.

We miss you, Caroline, said Pip. *We'll take care of that thing.*

"I know you will, Pip," said vision-of-Caroline. "Remember. You must try. That's all. And then you'll move on. We're together through time." Her image started to fade, like a mist absorbed into the air.

Then the space within the pyramid was clear. Not a foggy spot.

They dared not step inside, at the moment. Esme leaned down to touch a cat, as if to ground herself in a three-dimensional, organic creature. Simon put a hand on Pip's soft neck. Sherman came over and leaned into Esme's leg. Carl boldly flew to the top of the pyramid and crowed, triumphant. Like the blaring of Tibetan trumpets across the Himalayas.

What they didn't know was that Caroline had had a vision, just months ago, in her meditation shed. She sat on her platform on a thick cotton mattress covered with an ornate bedspread, colored yellow as the dominant color. It was two o'clock. She could hear a mild drizzle outside because three of four windows were open, letting in the warming spring air. She'd lit a few candles, scented pear and freesia, to evoke the smells of blossoms early in the season.

While in meditation, her mind was transported to a scene not wholly unfamiliar: a school in the Annapurna Valley of Nepal. The settlement was rustic and could be reached only by walking up and down steep valleys on stone steps, crafted by hand over decades. They were like ladders across the countryside. The area was so remote that all supplies, for building and living, were carried in on the backs of porters and donkeys. Some produce was farmed on tiny plateaus on hillsides. Protein came from chicken eggs, cow and goat milk made into yogurt. Most of the residents were Buddhist and ate lentils and rice primarily.

"Will Ananda Ma come back?" asked a female child's voice. ("Ma" was a respectful form of address.)

They were inside a mud-walled room with a tin roof. There were benches and sleeping platforms scattered through the room, and a primitive kerosene stove in the corner, with kitchen pots and utensils.

Ananda, Caroline thought. What a pretty name meaning "eternal joy" and "bliss."

She became aware of a woman lying on a cot along one wall, on her back. She was covered with a thick, hand-woven wool blanket. There was a cloth on her forehead, saturated with something.

"She may not," said a voice out of sight, near the stove. "She's been in a coma so long that I fear she may choose not to return. Ektaa, please freshen the compress."

The girl got up from a stool. Beside her, a large black hill dog sat up. In Nepali, he was a Pahari Kukur--having a long furry coat, looking like a black bear, with brown patches on his head and eyes. There were tan spots on his feet and stomach. His

normal job was protecting livestock and herding sheep, but he was a loyal protector of humans too. The girl Ektaa--"unity"-- dipped the compress in a mud pot and squeezed excess liquid from it, before placing it on Ananda's brow.

"I will miss her so much," said a boy. "Who'll run the school if she doesn't recover?"

"Soumi, it's very hard to find a headmistress willing to stay here. We do our best."

Soumi--"soft-natured"-- was slightly smaller than the girl. He sat cross legged near the feet of Ananda. They had been there for days. The room was stuffy, being kept warm by closing the windows to cold air from outside.

Caroline received the thought: "You're needed as a walk-in. Ananda is tired and her spirit longs for relief from this life. Her body is still good. Her mission here is precious: she teaches a hundred children from the whole valley. Some of them walk the stone steps for hours to come to school. They'll love you, and you'll save many of them from the worst poverty and hard lives. You'll lift a hundred souls by your presence, every day."

She knew of this form of reincarnation. It was a solution for unusual circumstances, where a soul becomes despondent, or, when a soul feels simply done with a karmic mission and ready to move on. The person that was Ananda would have no inkling that a "soul transplant" had occurred. She would simply feel renewed, and the walk-in would start a new life in the middle, instead of the beginning, of a life journey. Each soul had different missions in life, with a little overlap, but they were fulfilled sharing the same body, in sequence, however.

"Do you accept?" asked the thought in Caroline.

Was she ready to leave Sedro Woolley? Had she done enough there? Was she finished, her business settled, things put in place as her legacy? Yes, she thought. The one piece of unfinished business--protecting the contents of the Indian-gods lunch box-- was a task she could leave to the Cabal.

She looked at the girl Ektaa and the boy Soumi and remembered Esme and Simon. Even a devoted black dog! They were part of a soul family that traveled together through eons of time. One incarnation was not the first or last time they would share sentient lives. She would return to Buddhist lands.

"Yes," she thought. "I accept."

Ananda, a woman in her early forties, stirred under the wool blanket. One arm pushed the cover away from her chin.

"Look!" Soumi exclaimed. "Look!"

She opened her eyes and looked around the dark room, the three faces close by. Her face was pale, but color was returning. "Ektaa, my dear," she said, turning to the girl who'd just put a new compress on her brow. "Thank you."

Ektaa burst into tears of joy.

Flight

THE FRONT DOORBELL RANG. It rang so seldom that everyone in the family had to think about it before they figured out what the sound was. It was early on Saturday.

Molly was in the shower. She heard it, but assumed that Esme or Simon would answer the door.

Esme peaked from the side of the upstairs window and saw a gray Ford Escort parked in front. When she leaned close, she could see the top of a head. It was Mrs. Dinsdale.

Simon was in his room.

Esme grabbed her school backpack and emptied it of books. She fished in a bin of miscellaneous belongings and brought up a headlamp. A hoodie lying on the end of her bed got stuffed into the bag. Then she rushed to Simon's room with her sneakers in hand.

"Simon, quick," she whispered. "In the name of Lopez Island, we've got to get out of here. Grab your hoodie, find a flash light. Get your shoes. We've gotta run. People are after us!"

He'd seen Esme in her commando mode before and didn't ask questions. His shoes were next to the bed. He also grabbed his hoodie, found the headlamp hanging on the dresser knob.

The front doorbell rang again. And again, as they stepped quietly down the stairs and into the kitchen. Esme grabbed a jar of peanut butter, some bottles of water, some apples and a bag of trail mix. Pip was startled in his bed in the kitchen, near the door. She looked at him and grabbed a large bag of dog biscuits. Sherman must have been zonked on Molly's bed, and Esme didn't call him. He wasn't eager for arduous walks, in any case.

"Are you going to get that?" shouted Molly from the bathroom on the first floor. "Esme?"

The doorbell rang again.

The three quietly opened the back door and snuck out. They ran across the back yard and into the woods.

It took about half an hour to get to the hospital grounds. They knew their way around. Esme steered them to a structure farthest from the parking lot for tourists, walkers, and frisbee golf players. There were only a few people walking around that far, even on a good weekend. All the signs said "do not enter buildings" so they did not tend to go deep, to get interesting photos. Boards were falling. Spider webs. Rotted wood, rusted pipes, mud from occasionally flooded floors.

They settled against the outside of a back wall, in the soft weeds, behind bushes. It was late in October, still warm. They had just gotten back from school that day.

"What's up?" asked Simon.

"The social services lady. She might have been looking to take us away. We can't risk that."

"Why?"

"They don't like us. They want to bug Mom and Dad."

"Where do they take us?"

"Places like this, Simon. They put kids away that need to be fixed. Then they try to fix us."

"How do you know?"

"I read about indigenous people. Missionaries abducted them and put them in camps. They made them dress in white kid's clothes and pray, and do chores. They cut their hair. They tried to convert them. They're cruel. They beat the kids."

"Man, Esme. That's no good!"

"I know, right? We can't count on Mom and Dad fighting them off. We're like an native nation. Out-numbered."

"How long do we have to stay away?"

"Until it looks like they've given up on us. I think a few days, at least."

"Are we staying right here?"

"I think we should go deeper into the woods, just to be safe. Do you think you'll be okay doing that?"

He shrugged. "For sure." They often went on night hikes. The woods at night were familiar. But he might miss his book, and the little army of plastic super-heros waiting for him to put them into action.

It started to rain, so they moved inside the ruins of a building. Pip huddled up against Simon. Esme gave the dog a few biscuits. She and Simon ate an apple. As the rain intensified, they put on their hoodies, to stay warm.

It was a long night, with intermittent downpours. They stayed dry, but the late October night was almost too chilly for their hoodies.

In the morning, they got up and headed away from the hospital grounds, toward the dense woods. It wasn't as familiar as the grounds, but they knew where they were, and houses and roads were left behind. All the greenery was soaking wet, not just damp with dew. Their jeans got wet although they were walking deer trails with some clearance. Pip ran ahead a few feet, almost like a guide.

They walked a long time. Esme got a little concerned about leaving familiar territory, but figured Pip would help them find their way back. They stopped for another apple, peanut butter, and dog biscuit. It started to rain again.

"Shouldn't we stop, Esme?" asked Simon. "Far enough?"

"I don't know. Let's wait for a clearing and see what it looks like."

The rain turned into a fierce storm, with thunder and lightning. All three were soaked, plodding step by step along a narrow muddy path. They came on the side of a river--probably a stream that fed into Hanson Creek, past the Upper Skagit Reservation. They were hiking uphill now, toward Lyman Hill. There was a clearing alongside the creek, a giant sand bar.

Pip ran out on the bar, to get a drink from the river.

Just then a flash of lightning went off, six feet in diameter, like a bomb in the air, right above him.

The children screamed and screamed, louder than ever in their lives. They'd never seen anything like it. "Pip! Pip! Pip!" they shouted. They were both shaking and squatted down in place. There was no answer from the little dog.

Esme sobbed into her trembling hands, weak from the fright of the bomb. Simon was literally struck dumb. After a few minutes, Esme got up.

Pip's body was on the sand bar, prone, like he'd relaxed into a nap on his side. His eyes were closed. Esme knelt beside him and put a hand on his shoulder. His fur was wet but his body was still warm. She sobbed and sobbed. Simon stood near, tears streaming into the rain water dripping down his cheeks. They both knew Pip was gone.

Finally, Esme stood up. Oblivious to the rain, she pulled off her wet hoodie. She draped it on the wet pebbles of the sandbar next to Pip, then slowly and gently moved the twelve-pound dog's body onto the cloth. Then she wrapped it around him like swaddling a baby, and lifted him into her arms.

The two kids looked at each other. It was as if they were standing in a shower. Simon put his hand on the cloth where Pip's head was.

Pip was as old as they were. He too had been a little confused with the logistics of living in two houses. But he was a constant between them, like a third child. The cats had stayed with Molly, but Pip braved finding new warm spots to snooze in Donald's house, calming to the new set of sounds: the dishwasher, the furnace, the opening and closing of front and back doors. At night, new spaces that were lit by lamps or dark, some unfamiliar, scary corners and closets. Finding his food dish when he woke up and forgot where he was. He always knew where Esme and Simon were.

Where did that personality, that soul, go? How could this wet and cold, heavy, black blob of fur be Pip? Where was the bounce, the quick lick of assurance?

"We better get off this sandbar, Simon," Esme said with a weak voice.

They turned back into the woods. Without Pip running ahead, it wasn't clear where they needed to go, so they just walked along the deer trail they'd been on when it turned toward the river. Now they wandered, unthinking, and paying little attention to where they were.

After another hour they were dragging their feet but still in the middle of woods and dense undergrowth, with no stony outcrops for shelter in sight.

A scrawny full-size German short-haired pointer appeared directly in their path, heading toward them. He did not look like a dog who saw many treats but could probably hunt squirrels if he needed to. He looked like a dog might, who was looking for a bone he'd put down some time ago, and just remembered where that was. Nonchalant. They knew him and his dark brown head, speckled body. It was Jackson. They almost never saw him, the last time being at the stoning of Simon.

Come this way, he said. He turned around on the narrow path and looked behind him to see if they got the message.

Esme sighed, giving up the struggle to stay strong. She'd follow, just fine. Wherever. Pip's twelve pounds were getting heavy. Her t-shirt was soaked through and cold. Her sneakers squished.

In about fifteen minutes they came up on the front porch of a cabin. There, smoking a pipe, sat a man she recognized as Trollop.

He put his pipe on a barrel next to his chair and got up. Then he eased himself down a few wet stairs, careful with his feet. Esme could see his hand with the missing fingers on the banister, but nothing like that mattered.

Trollop came up to her and reached for Pip's body with his creepy hands. "We'll rest him on the porch if you don't mind," he said. He didn't even ask what it was. He took up the bundle and went back up the stairs. Esme could see that he wasn't weak, just careful and deliberate. He went toward the end of the porch and placed the bundle on the deck, out of the rain, but off to the side.

"Y'all need to get dry," he said, looking over his shoulder. He headed into his cabin.

They got their own feet to move up the wooden stairs, holding onto a dripping banister. Wood can be slippery, they knew. They stopped at the door. Inside was dark except for an oil lamp. It was cluttered but not crazy; he was not a hoarder. There were a few benches, a table, a crude kitchen with a wash basin and a camping stove for cooking. A few tin dishes were clearly drying after being washed. There was a stash of cans on a shelf, and a pot that looked like it was full of a stew of some kind. A wood stove seemed to have live coals in it, keeping it going for cooking if not for heat. He added some chopped firewood to stoke it and a warm fire flared up eager to do its job.

Esme watched the flames and swallowed. Fire was not their friend, right now.

"I'll get you some shirts. We'll let your clothes get dry." He went to a small cabinet and came back with two large sweatshirts. They were so large that no other clothing was needed. "Change over there behind the door."

The door was open to a storage room of sorts. Esme could see a few guns in the corner. There was room to stand in the closet and change. They took turns.

Trollop pulled two chairs near the stove and put their wet clothes out to dry. He motioned toward a few benches along the wall. He'd cleared off things.

They sat and rolled up the long sleeves on each arm. They'd been chilled for days, and the sweatshirts still had enough fleece inside to feel delicious.

"Only rabbit stew, although I have sardines if you want," he stood before them.

"Stew, thanks," said Esme.

"Stew," said Simon, nodding. He started crying.

Trollop ignored him and put some of the stew into a smaller pan, lit the gas hotplate, and put the pan on. He got some bread out of a large canister and sliced off a few pieces. He got some cheese out of a smaller plastic box and cut pieces. He handed them each a wide-lipped tin bowl.

Esme started crying too.

"The stew ain't that bad," said Trollop.

She nodded.

Jackson had followed them inside and spread himself on a big pad in the corner. He had a few chew bones stashed around his bed and sniffed around to see which one seemed right for now.

"There are dog biscuits in my pack," said Esme, choking on the words.

She put her bowl down on the bench beside her and got the biscuits from her pack. She walked over to Jackson and put a bunch near his nose, next to his bed. *Thank you*, she said.

Jackson seemed to smile.

"Now there's a spot of happy," said Trollop, looking at his dog. He sat down in a large home-made chair with arms and giant cushions, and got out another pipe while the stew heated up.

"It's going to rain all night," he said. "I'll walk you back in the a.m. Right?"

Esme and Simon nodded.

The idea of going back suddenly got real in Esme's mind. "Mr. Trollop," she said quietly, "We don't really want to go back."

"How so?" he asked, taking a puff on the pipe.

"They're going to lock us up."

"Who says?"

"I just know it. They're trashing Caroline, the lady who died. She was my godmother. They hate my parents. They think Simon's an alien." She stopped eating and stared into her bowl.

"Oh my." Trollop took a puff. "Where do you think they are going to lock you up?"

She looked him in the eye. He was, after all, one of those people who had been put away. And then after that, he ran like hell and disappeared into the woods.

"Foster care, maybe. Some prison for kids, maybe, where they aren't nice to you. They get money for keeping you in a pen. Away from your parents."

"What makes you think they're going to take you?"

"The lady was coming to the house. On a Saturday. So people won't see you taken from school."

"Baby, it's not all bad. We live in a big world. Maybe she was just making a visit she is required to make, and wanted to see your family at home."

"You got put in the hospital!" Esme pulled the stops here.

He chuckled. "I was a mess, girl. You're not a mess. Neither is junior, here." He smiled at Simon who was locked on every word.

"Simon nearly got killed, you know."

"I know."

Esme pondered that. How did he know?

"Well," she said, "It could happen."

"But he survived that crazy day. You will survive many crazy days, in your life. You gotta move on. Tough it to the next one."

Esme squirmed in her chair. She took up another spoonful of stew.

"Why can't we stay here?" she asked. "Caroline lived in a cave for years. People are too awful."

"You don't belong in a cave, Esme."

After they had their stew and bread and cheese, they settled under a few woolen blankets on another pad bigger than Jackson's, on the floor in another corner of the room.

Esme whispered to Simon, "Can you bring Pip back, Simon?"

"No," he whispered back. "I'm pretty sure." He put his hand to his brow, as if to retrieve any idea buried in his head somewhere.

They both wished Pleiadians on Earth had a few more magical powers. Sure, the soul is infinite and as part of Pip's soul group they would meet in other carnations. But, from the human perspective, it hurt. One of the purposes of reincarnation was to experience emotions and the messy ups and downs of a life on Earth. Well, okay, they felt the pain. It was painful. An infinite soul may not cry, but a human, especially in bewildering and vulnerable childhood, was going to cry a lot.

Trollop had a wooden bunk in a far corner of the L-shaped cabin. It had a big window next to it, so he could see out into the woods, and, let his pipe smoke drift away from the cabin through the open gap. He seemed to be reading by a small light late into the night, but the two drifters were deep in oblivion early on.

In the morning, Esme woke to the smell of coffee. She watched the back of Trollop wearing a long heavy flannel shirt over his jeans. Without the knit hat, his hair was a wild mess, as if he really didn't care to tame it, ever. Simon was still in a deep sleep. Jackson came in from outside, through the door that was partly ajar. The rain had stopped and the air was warmer than yesterday.

"Outhouse around the right side," said Trollop, not turning around.

Esme got up and found her shoes by the stove. Things had dried to a tolerable point overnight.

Trollop had made them oatmeal with chocolate powder and berries, and hot chocolate. Esme wondered where he got supplies like that, but it was amazing and wonderful after two days of hunger and chill. The two sat side by side on a bench up against a small table.

When they seemed to be finished eating, Trollop went into the storage room and came back. Esme turned around. He was holding a lunch box. With Hindu gods painted on it.

"Hey! Hey! What?" she shouted, jumping up from the bench. "You have it! How? How?" She took a few extra jumps to tame the jolt of energy through her little body.

"I didn't think it was safe where you left it. I'm sorry, Esme." He held it out to her.

She took it up like a box of treasure and stared at it.

"Do you know what's in it, Esme?" he asked.

"No. No, I don't," she spoke to the tin box. "I just know Caroline was keeping it safe from strangers."

"You can't keep it forever, you know. It's important for other people to take a look. You know?" He was calm.

"No. What people?"

"Science people. It's possibly related to aliens. Did you know?"

"No." She looked at Simon. "How do you know? Did you look inside?"

"No, I didn't. I just got a feeling. A feeling that maybe Caroline sent to me. You understand what I'm saying?"

"Caroline told you?"

"In a manner of speaking," he chuckled. "I don't think you need to guard it the rest of your life, Esme. It might be better if the authorities got it."

"Authorities?" He didn't trust any authorities himself. Why should she?

"Why don't we trust that your Caroline is pointing the way to give it up. Why don't we trust that she'll keep it from all hellish shenanigans? And keep us from all hellish shenanigans."

Esme put the box to her chest. She looked at Simon for some signal. Would he agree to just "let it go?" She was puzzled by Trollop. People said that once, he'd been beaten by a guard at the hospital. The same guard kicked and beat another man to death, and five physicians testified that the man had died of epilepsy. The patient who witnessed the beating testified, and he was discounted. The guard was acquitted of manslaughter. Trust was a strong word for Trollop to use.

Back at their house, or rather, Caroline's old house, a lady stood on the porch. "Hello, I'm Florence Dinsdale, from the Child Welfare Services."

Molly had finally gotten out of her shower and made it to the door. Clearly the kids hadn't answered the door. "May I ask why you're here?" She'd heard about Esme's interrogation at school.

"Just checking on the kids. You know, it's my job."

"I see. And of all the kids in Sedro Woolley, why are you worried about mine?" Molly didn't move away from the door.

"Well there were a few incidents that were unusual. We like to follow up." Florence smiled benignly.

"I don't think that's necessary. We're quite fine here." Molly kept a hand on the partially open door.

"May I see the kids, just for a minute? It's procedure."

"Not really. It's not convenient."

"Well, I really don't mean to impose, but that might require another follow up, and an escalation of attention, if you know what I mean."

"I don't know what you mean."

"A conference at the school, at a minimum."

"I see." Molly moved away from the door. "Just a minute and I'll call them." She left the lady standing on the porch, pushed the door mostly closed, and went to the stairwell. "Esme, Simon. Can you come down for a minute?" She looked up the stairwell. There was no response. "Esme, Simon, can you hear me? I need you to come down for a minute."

Getting no response, she glanced back at the front door to see if the lady was staying put, and went up the stairs. Neither child was in their bedroom. She remembered that they were home when she went into the shower. "Esme! Simon!"

Molly returned to the front door. "I'm sorry, Mrs. Dinsdale, they seem to have gone out to play. It'll have to be another time."

"Are you sure they're not here?"

"I'm sure. They're free to play in the woods when they want. They're just not here now." She moved the door toward closing.

"Ah well, I'll try again. Thanks for your time." Florence turned and went down the stairs of the porch toward her car.

Molly went back upstairs to confirm that they weren't there. Then she called Donald on his cell phone. "Don, are the kids with you? They're not here."

"No, they're not. I'm at work."

"We just had a visit from Child Welfare Services. She wanted to see the kids. 'Just checking,' she said."

"What! That's outrageous! What're they doing in our business?" Don's voice headed for a roar.

"I know. She threatened to 'escalate attention.' I decided to call them to just show up, but they aren't here. They were here just a minute ago."

"Give'em a little time. You know they go out and about. Call me if they're not back soon."

"Okay. Okay." Molly paused. "Later. Bye." She hung up, sat down, and hugged herself.

Donald called at 7 pm that night. "Back yet?"

"No. Also, Pip's gone."

"I'm coming over. I can go out and check some of their places."

Molly saw his car pull up in front. He waved at her and headed into the back yard, carrying a flash light.

Two hours later he called. "Back yet?" It had started raining hard. He hadn't brought an umbrella.

"No. Where are you?" she asked.

"Heading back. We have to decide what to do."

"I know." She hung up and made some tea. She looked over at the cats Persephone and Penelope. "What do you think?" She said to them.

They sat impervious. *Shall we rat on the runaways?* Persephone looked at Penelope.

Nope. They'll be all right. They've got Pip too, Penelope answered.

Donald came into the house, soaked to the skin. Molly gave him a cup of hot soup.

"If we call the police, we walk right into Child Welfare Services. If we don't, we risk them to exposure, or whatever. What do you think is going on?" Donald asked.

"Esme knew the woman from that awful interview at school. She might have just run away."

"In that case, she knows what she's doing. I think they'll come back."

213

"How long should we wait?" Molly started fussing with things on the kitchen counter, pushing them into proper places.

"In this rain, they might be under shelter somewhere. And it's pitch dark. Let's give them the night. What do you think?"

"Oh Don," she put her hands to her mouth. "Really?"

"Really. They're resourceful kids, Molly. If we call the police, you know there'll be a big search through the night. Mobs of people involved. Maybe helicopters. Attention. And it might just end up finding them in a vacant building. And that could still take all night."

"I'm so worried." She accepted his hug. It had been weeks since they'd even touched.

"I'll stay over. I don't have to work tomorrow. I'll sleep on the couch. Okay?" He held her gently, not to disturb the hug.

"I'll get you some bedding." Molly pulled away and went to the linen closet for blankets and pillow.

They next morning they were both bleary from lack of sleep. There were no kids back in the house. They waited to act, hopeful to hear the back door open and clear all worry away.

Instead, the front door bell rang again. Molly could see through the corner of the window that now there were two cars out front: a police car, and Florence Dinsdale.

"Hello again, Mrs. Jenson," began Florence. "I told you I might be back to see the children. I wondered if they were home now."

"How ya doing, Molly," said Officer Kameron over her shoulder.

"And why are you here again? I assured you that everything's all right. You've seen Esme in school. This is uncalled-for." She looked at Kameron with a silent plea for sanity.

"But they weren't home. And I'm just doing my job. Checking to see if everything is all right here. Child welfare."

Molly stepped out onto the porch. "You just want to take kids away. You have no cause to be bothering us."

"Oh no, we're not taking anybody's kids away. We're just checking the home."

"My eye," said Molly, hanging onto the door behind her. "Missionaries have been stealing brown babies all over the world, forever. Millions. Putting them in camps and institutions to 'save' them, and 'fix' them. Indigenous people, aborigines, Samis--you take'em and break'em, and send them back, and then you say they're no good. You mess them up under some preposterous mission to save their souls." Molly stopped to catch her breath. "If there's a sin, that's it! Harvesting souls. Brown babies ..."

"Whoa, Molly, wait a minute," Kameron stepped forward pushing Florence aside. "Nothing like that is happening here. This is a routine visit."

"And what's your routine? Huh? What makes you think there's anything wrong here?" Molly clutched the neck of her blouse.

By now Donald had squeezed through the partially open door behind Molly and stood on the porch. He put a hand on her arm.

"Now, Molly," said Kameron, "Please be reasonable. Just let the lady see the kids for a minute and we're out of here."

"Well they're not here," said Molly looking at Don.

"Where are they?" Kameron asked.

"Gone," said Don, calmly.

"You made them run away yesterday!" Molly raised her voice, looking at Florence. "You threaten them, and now they're in trouble! It's because of you!"

"Since yesterday?" Kameron looked at Florence. "All night?"

"Yes, all night," said Don. "They know their way around the woods, to be sure. We're still waiting for them to come back."

"But they're not here," said Kameron.

By now, Florence had stepped back more than a few feet, looking embarrassed and upset.

"Well let's get some people to go look for them, Molly, and Don. Is that okay?" Kameron said.

"It rained all night," said Don, "They might have found a place to shelter."

"In any case, we'll go looking. The weather's going to be bad all day. We need to go look."

"Okay," said Don, putting his arm around Molly.

As expected, Officer Kameron called out several police cars and a dozen people to fan out from the house in an organized search. By the end of the day, people had reached the grounds of the hospital and found nothing. It was still raining, and in the afternoon, a lightning storm came in. Many retreated from exposure to that. They called off the search at nightfall. The house was full of people reporting back, coming for coffee, water, donated sandwiches. Molly and Donald could barely keep up with unrelenting conversations that all centered on worry and speculation.

Molly thought about the irony of having all kinds of strangers in the house now, instead of Florence Dinsdale. All they needed was a mob of judgmental people, casing out their house and snooping. Nobody was mean that way, but she was painfully aware of being surrounded by intruders.

Kameron had become some kind of ally; he pushed people away from the two parents and fended off the well-intended, but overwhelming commiseration from neighbors.

That night, Donald joined Molly on their old bed, with his arm on her, as they tossed and turned through a second night.

Down From Lyman Hill

THE TREK DOWN FROM LYMAN HILL took hours. Blessedly, it had stopped raining, and their clothes were dry. Pip's body was stiff by now, and Trollop cradled him in a sling across his front, the way he might carry rabbits he'd just shot. Jackson proudly led the way, looking back often, with encouragement to get a move on. They avoided roads until they were about half a mile from home. Then, Trollop moved the sling from his shoulder to Esme's. She passed the Hindu lunch-box to Simon. Their shoes were muddy and still damp. Nothing a washing machine wouldn't cure.

"I leave you to it, kiddoos," said Trollop. "I think you know Pip's in a good place. Right?"

Esme swallowed back a sob. She nodded and looked at Simon. He nodded too.

Trollop waved his gruesome fingerless right hand as if he were cheering a sports team. He reached down to stroke Jackson's ear next to his thigh.

"Thank you, Mr. Trollop," said Esme. "You're awesome. We'll bring you some chocolate one of these days."

He laughed. Esme backed away from him, wanting to remember the navy knitted hat pulled low over his ears (no matter the weather), the generous brown flannel shirt, the heavy clumped jeans over dirty workman's boots. His face was clean, though, and shining with satisfaction.

They started down the shoulder of the road to their house. Within hundreds of feet of their house, people spotted them, and a dozen came running toward them. The shouting brought Molly and Donald dashing out of the house.

The children's hair was in extreme tangle: it had been rained on, dried, slept on. No one carried a comb. Trollop certainly hadn't thought to find one, if he even had one himself. Their clothes were muddy and torn. In fact, they looked like Trollop's children might, living on the wild side.

"Esme! Simon!" Everyone was crying. Even Officer Kameron was pretending to wipe his brow. There were group hugs, over and over.

Suddenly, Donald stuttered, "Esme, the sling!" He put his hand on it. "Oh my God! Oh my God! No!" He burst into fresh tears to the back of his hand and looked over at Molly.

"Really? Pip? No. No." She cried.

"Lightning," said Simon. "In one second." He placed a hand on the sling too.

Then they took notice of the lunch-box. "What's this?" asked Don, pulling his face back into attention.

"It's a lunch box, Dad. It was Caroline's," said Simon.

"Where'd you get it?"

"Never mind." Esme took it from Simon and looked at Officer Kameron. "Here. There are people looking for this. Caroline's. Don't open it. Oxygen might destroy the contents."

Kameron took it, puzzled. "People?"

"Science people. Area 51 types. You've heard of them?"

His eyes grew wide. He looked around the crowd to see if anyone recognized the phrase. No one so much as blinked.

"OOO-kay," he said. He paused. "Roger that." He tightened his grip on the handle. "Glad to see you two. We looked everywhere."

"I'm sorry," said Esme. "You keep Mrs. Dinsdale away from us. Or we'll have to go live in a stump house." She looked him in the eye.

"Stump house?" He stepped back. "You just stay put, Esme. Put in a few years here, and then you can get yourself an RV and get the hell out. Hear me?"

Esme chuckled. She'd heard her mother say that every other old lady in Sedro Woolley was saving her money to get an RV and get the hell out. Their "vision boards," on the back of a pantry door out of sight of husbands and snoopy neighbors, held photos of favorite RV models, and maps of places they would go. Social Security was going to be enough to pay for gas and food. Indeed, some of the local ladies' book clubs were just an excuse to get together, drink some wine, and share tips and particulars about the RV life. Ladies did not need to gather in a bar for this kind of fun, sharing a dream of flight.

The "lost children" made the news. After seeing their pictures in the *Sedro Sentinel*, many people in town recognized them and Donald and Molly by sight, and made a point of coming up to them, and telling them where they were "when they heard what happened," and how glad they were that everyone was all right. Casseroles appeared for days, from a church ladies' club. The citizens of Sedro Woolley were mostly proud of themselves for a successful rally, for their community spirit, for feeling as if they'd saved the children. They certainly responded as if these two children were their own. The celebratory mood lasted for months until other news bumped it into town history.

PART THREE: IT GETS BETTER

The Box

OFFICER KAMERON CALLED DONALD and told him that the people who had received the "treasure box" were extremely grateful, and they invited the family to come and visit and see what the "treasure" was. The visit had to be secret, and no leaking any stories.

Donald and Molly were still puzzled about the box.

"Kids, what was in it?" they asked.

Simon let Esme answer. "Um, Caroline came across it in the woods. She'd seen a small UFO crash, she said. There were things scattered around. She figured that the aliens would not want to be discovered, so she did not report it. In fact, she said, she left the place alone. In a few days, she said, another UFO came by. She thought they were cleaning up or something. After they left, she went to the exact place. They'd forgotten something. She didn't say what it was, except that she could tell it was most precious and she needed to protect it. That's what she kept in the lunch box."

"Why did you think it needed to be kept a secret?"

"Because Caroline said it needed to be a secret. She said the Area 51 people took things related to UFOs and hid them from everybody, and lied about them. Also, she said it was sacred and she didn't think it should end up in a research lab or a museum. She said it was like the remains of Native Americans, and

225

Egyptians, that were taken far away by conquerors and put on display as souvenirs, and then they were used to make things up about the dead."

Molly rubbed her cheek. "But you gave it up. It's not sacred anymore? Or you trust the authorities to treat it with respect?"

"Oh no," piped up Simon. He looked at Esme with alarm.

"We, um, thought about it," said Esme. She waited for Simon to settle down and look like he knew what she was going to say. "We had to give it up. We couldn't keep it forever." The two of them remembered Trollop's advice.

"Well," said Donald, "Officer Kameron is coming on Saturday to take us to a secure military bunker in Bellingham. We'll have a field trip! What do you think?"

"Wow," said Simon. "So cool."

The ride to Bellingham in Kameron's police car was exciting enough for Simon and Esme. They felt very important. They'd told the Cabal they were going and would report back. It was a big day--the culmination of their mission to rescue the lunch box from the very start.

In mid-November, the police car drove over half an hour toward Bellingham and finally, far east outside of town where the houses thinned out, took a small country road for fifteen minutes, and then went down a narrow forest road to a guard station, a complete little shack with windows and a roof, were a soldier could sit warm and comfortable. There was a heavy metal gate on the road, and chain-link fence about eight feet high, with four rows of barbed wire strung on top of that. It didn't look like it belonged in the woods at all. The soldier was not stern at all, since he was expecting Officer Kameron and the passengers. He asked everyone to get out of the car and checked to see that nobody else was hiding inside. All four of the Jensens were reserved. Officer Kameron, on the other hand, was jovial. "Never would have found the place, I assure you, without your special instructions," he said to the guard.

"Well, it's a secure site. Not that many people visit, for sure," said the tall, skinny soldier. He was not holding a rifle, but he did have a holster with a gun in it, as did Officer Kameron. "You just go ahead to the first building and park in front. I'll tell'm you're here."

"Right-o," said Kameron.

They were met by a woman in a lab coat, not a soldier. "I'm so glad to meet you!" she said, as she shook hands with Donald, Molly, Esme, and Simon. Then she shook hands with Officer Kameron. "Thanks for bringing them out. We really appreciate their giving up the object. Not everybody is so generous. A lot of people want to hoard things like that as souvenirs, and then they turn up a hundred years down the road. By the way, I'm Dr. Teleman."

"What kind of doctor are you?" asked Esme.

"Why, I'm a biological archaeologist, my dear. We study ancient skeletal remains. These days, we do a lot of genetic analyses."

"Does that mean this thing had skeletal remains?" asked Molly.

"Not necessarily. But we hope for organic material of some kind. Let's go into the conference room."

The five visitors sat in five chairs along a long table, with Dr. Teleman on the other side. She was joined by a young soldier, clearly an assistant in the way he deferred to her.

She placed the lunch box on the table in front of them. "I wanted to give you the experience of opening the lunch box yourselves. I don't know if you ever did. Did you?" She looked at Esme and Simon. It might have been a trick question. She was a pro.

"No, no. Of course not," said Esme. "Caroline warned us it would hurt the contents."

"Nope," said Simon.

"The young lady advised me that exposure to the air was bad," added Officer Kameron.

"Of course, we can't tell if you did. The latch simply comes open as if you had a lunch in there. It wasn't really sealed in any special way. Not even to keep a lunch fresh!" she chuckled.

She unlatched it, and slowly opened it in the middle of the table.

"OH!" they exclaimed in unison.

The object inside was nothing any of them had ever seen. It was long, swaddled in a brown cloth, with a shriveled lump of a head clearing the top. It was placed diagonally in the box.

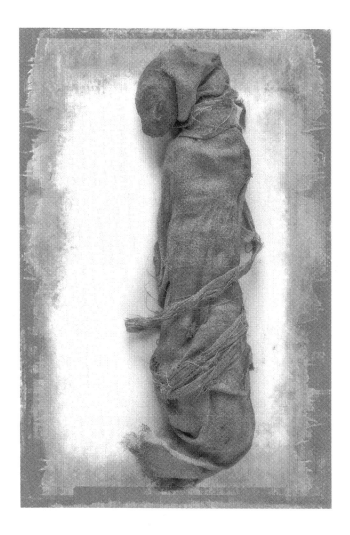

"What is it?" asked Donald. He looked at Esme and Simon to see if they acted like they recognized it.

Dr. Teleman behaved like a magician about to reveal a trick. After the assistant put a clean white cotton cloth on the table beside the box, she lifted the object out and placed it there. It was like swaddled baby, only skinny and long. "It's a mummified kitten! We did an X-ray, and we took a sample of tissue where there was some left. It's a kitten maybe six weeks old. Mummified in the classic Egyptian manner."

Kameron and the two kids looked at each other. They expected body parts. Body parts of an alien, really. Dried up, gray, metallic, gruesome looking. Formerly organic stuff in an unrecognizable shape. A smell, maybe. Shriveled skin. Or a peculiar metal object, a piece of a spaceship.

"What??" Donald was playing head of the family.

"You can't see the ears. They're under the wrapping. But they're individually wrapped too." The Doctor pointed at the ears.

"What's an Egyptian mummy doing in Sedro Woolley?" asked Kameron.

"I haven't a clue," said Teleman. "If you have any ideas, tell me." She looked at the kids. "The ancient Egyptians believed that mummifying a pet would make its soul live forever. Some of the animals were sacrificed so they could play the role of a messenger between mortals and gods. But also, at least one Egyptian god, Ra, is depicted as a cat. We don't know if this is a god figure, or a pet that was sent on a divine mission. A sacred cat."

"What's under the cloth?" asked Molly.

"Mostly more cloth, filling the dried body. Sometimes the mummies have eyes drawn them, or have colored glass, obsidian, or rock crystal put in the eye sockets. This one has no other adornments. The genetic material we got was from inside the head. We could stick a needle in there."

Simon choked and put his head in his hands.

"Can we touch it?" asked Esme. She put a hand on Simon's arm.

"Well yes, gently. I would think you deserve to be allowed to do that. In the least. It won't be handled much once we put it into storage with controlled air."

Esme pressed Simon's arm. They were side by side. They leaned forward together, and each placed a hand flat on the body of the kitten.

It's encoded, she signaled to Simon, keeping her face directed at the mummy, her expression locked on innocence.

"Greetings. I am from the Pleiades, Taygeta. We Pleiadians come to you from the future. We are here to offer our assistance in raising your vibrations. Know that the Earth can be sustained-- humans and all other species--if you stop destructive practices. We have witnessed the mass extinction of mankind five times now. All of these were due to nature. The threat of another extinction is man-made and can be avoided. "

"That's cute," said Dr. Teleman, observing the two with their hands stretched out. "Kids are always so curious." She smiled at Donald and Molly.

She leaned over to pick up the mummy.

"Oh, no, please," said Esme. "Can we have another minute?"

"Well, of course, my dear. No problem." Teleman pulled away.

The two children closed their eyes to block out the distraction of staring adults. In silence, they 'heard:'

"I am a past incarnation of the pet you know as Pip. Just as we Pleiadians modified human DNA to increase the vibrations of your race, we introduced methods for messaging that transcend

231

human time. We gave the Egyptians the knowledge to preserve
the physical manifestation of certain light bodies."

Simon sighed and opened his eyes. Esme pulled her hand from the mummy and touched his arm in shared sadness. "Okay," she said. "Good-bye, little cat." She wished she could tell her Mom and Dad that they had just spoken to Pip, but it was just too complicated.

As Teleman then picked up the mummy and placed her back into the lunch box, she added, "Another thing, you guys. A mystery. The DNA of this cat is not normal. At least not for cats as we know them. There are genetic anomalies here. They don't match anything we know. Of course, in our human DNA, there are strands that we call 'junk DNA' because we don't know what it does. But we do know its patterns. The same in cats. This cat's 'junk DNA' is nothing we've seen before. In our lingo, there are no antecedents. That's another reason it's quite a precious specimen to have."

"Are you going to take her apart?" Simon asked.

"No, dear. We'll put her in a sterile container and she'll rest for a long time. Until somebody has some new knowledge that can explain her existence to us. Think of the storage like a columbarium. Do you know what that is?"

"No."

"It's a place where the ashes of the dead are placed in many cells, in a wall, or on shelves, for eternity. It's like a cemetery. It's sacred. It's respectful. Your kitten will have its own compartment, and rest there safe and sound from interference."

"You can call her Pip," said Esme.

Molly gasped.

Esme continued, "We just lost a dog called Pip. I think he would be her friend."

"All right, dear," said Dr. Teleman, closing the box. "I'll make a note of that. We often label our specimens. This one is 'Pip of Sedro Woolley.'"

That night, Esme visited Simon as he was falling asleep. "Do you think Trollop swapped out what was really in the lunch box?"

"I don't think so, Esme," he said. "But it's possible that there was another encoded-message-object in the box before this one. And he swapped it out for this one, for some reason."

"We'll never know." Esme paused. "But I liked Pip coming through."

"Trollop seemed to be in cahoots with Caroline, too," said Simon. He slipped away into a deep sleep.

What the Area 51 types missed out on, and didn't know, was a thing: a smart drone-like vehicle that gathered information about the earth by flying over and scanning an area. Whose size was small enough to fit in a standard-sized metal lunch box. Potentially, it could have given humans the knowledge of several technologies that were new to them, and very powerful: anti-gravity flight, massively smart surveillance, and inter-galactic signaling. Actually, even if contemporary humans had gotten their hands on it, it could take them a few centuries to unscramble or reverse engineer the technologies it represented. Still, the Pleiadians were not ready to hand it over to humans. Humans were showing that they couldn't handle nuclear power in safe and constructive ways; they were potentially on a path to destroy the Earth. Maybe future, saner generations, with higher vibrations and enlightenment, would receive these new powers, possibly through the intentional or accidental delivery of an object from space that would accelerate their discovery of new technologies.

A Piece of Tamanowas

AFTER CAROLINE DISAPPEARED, and the Cabal had managed to get the lunch box out of her shed, Trollop learned from Jackson where it was.

He waited a few weeks to send for the Pleiadian rescue squad. He placed a special combination of rocks on an outcropping within a quarter mile of his shack. Like crop circles and rock art all over the world, there were ways for signals to be sent and received from the galaxies. Some ancient tribes knew the techniques but they were generally kept secret and often died with the shaman or wizard who'd learned them.

Trollop had in his possession a ten-pound piece of lava rock carried from Tamanowas Rock near Port Townsend, Washington. "Tamanowas" means "spirit power" in the Klallam language. The Rock is a sacred site to the Coast Salish peoples and a pilgrimage site. What few people knew: it was also a potent extra-terrestrial signaling medium. The original Rock was full of crevices and dark deep pockets that were ideal for building up energies that needed a solid confined space. And, the Rock was connected, under layers of earth over many eons of time, to the arc of magma that had flowed across the Puget Sound area at one time. It was like an invisible black, porous highway threading the geography. Like quartz crystal, it had the property of being able to store the energy of a soul, including thoughts and feelings, and transmit them.

He created a cairn-like composition of stones, placing the ten-pound lava rock from Tamanowas in the center, surrounded by large pieces of shiny black obsidian, also a derivative of lava flows. The hard, glassy stone was good for making knives and arrow heads, but also good for reflection like a mirror. Trollop expected that the sun would bake and roast these rocks in a certain formation, heat them up like coals, glowing an invisible energy into the heavens. It could take days to work.

A week later his dog Jackson came out of the mossy forest behind his shack carrying a piece of something that looked like burnt charcoal. Trollop recognized it as Chaga mushroom, an exotic fungus that grows on birch trees and has magical properties. Trollop recognized that it was also serving as an encoded thought object. He touched it.

*The next full moon, on the crest of the same outcropping,
leave the Treasure. It will be retrieved.*

The full moon was five days away, he knew. He climbed
into the eaves of his cabin and retrieved the lunch box. Inside it
was a small round disk wrapped many times in burlap.

The kids knew Trollop as a former patient of the Northern
Hospital who never left the area after he was released when the
hospital closed. He was said to have PTSD from Vietnam, or, a
mountaineer who'd driven himself mad from times that got too
hard in Alaska. He was like a Yeti--lurking and hiding in the
woods, rarely seen, and even hard to spot. He was definitely not
eager to participate in "civilization," except to stop in a rustic
camping store to shop for basic provisions quickly, usually
involving a social interaction with another sympathetic
curmudgeon and maverick.

In fact, Trollop was a "walk in." He was a person whose
original soul had taken on more than it could handle, at some
point, and had opted to "trade" up with another soul: a generally
more advanced and hearty soul. (Like a heart transplant...) The
trade was a form of suicide for the original "owner," but also a
form of survival--basically a way for the original owner to
upgrade the "suit of meat" that is the human body and give it a
longer useful life on the planet Earth. This gave Trollop a special
role in earthly doings.

Five days later, at the designated time, he and Jackson
trudged up the hill to the special rock configuration. It was a
night hike, well-lit by the full moon. He placed the lunch box on
the rocks.

He was indeed in cahoots with Caroline. She had, on a similar night, been led to retrieve the object from a UFO that had to exit from Earth more quickly than it had planned.

The next day Trollop and Jackson returned to the spot. On top of the special rocks was the lunch box. Inside, he saw a burlap-wrapped object, but it was long and narrow, not a disk. He "read" its message and knew that it was a gift. Possibly it had been riding in a space craft for eons, or, it had been retrieved from the time-space grid, to give the humans something to treasure. A decoy, yes, but a pleasant one. A meaningful one. Mission accomplished.

Immortal Energy

MOLLY WAS THE FIRST IN THE FAMILY to spot the tiny news item in the *Sedro Sentinel*. She was disappointed that Raymond hadn't contacted her first; that she had to read about it like everyone else in Sedro Woolley. Maybe he was bored with the whole story by now.

"**A Puzzle Solved**

Thanks to Robert Spencer who was visiting family in Sedro Woolley and saw our appeal for help, we have the answer to the meaning of a message left behind by our departed neighbor, Caroline Milarep. He recognized the writing as Sanskrit, and the message is a quote from ancient texts:

हमारा शरीर प्रकाश है, हम अमर हैं।
Our body is light, we are immortal

हमारा शरीर प्यार है, हम अनन्त हैं।
Our body is love, we are eternal

RELATED BOOKS

Sedro-Woolley Historical Museum (2003). *Images of America: Sedro-Woolley Washington*

McGoffin, M.J. (2011). *Under the Red Roof: One Hundred Years at Northern State Hospital*

Winters, Randolph (1944). *The Pleiadian Mission: A Time of Awareness*

Marciniak, Barbara (1992). *Bringers of the Dawn: Teachings from the Pleiadians*

Rodwell, Mary (2002). *Awakening*

Cannon, Dolores (2001). *Convoluted Universe Book 1*

Cannon, Dolores (2011). *The Three Waves of Volunteers and the New Earth*

Cannon, Dolores (2015). *The Search for Hidden Sacred Knowledge*

Mendonca, Miguel and Barbara Lamb (2015). *Meet the Hybrids: The Lives and Missions of ET Ambassadors on Earth*

McTaggart, Lynne. (2001). *The Field: The Quest for the Secret Force of the Universe*

APPRECIATION

Thanks to Kathleen Sweeney who introduced me to Pleiadians.

To Paula Schaefer who enticed me to take a trip to Sedro Woolley where I found a treasure of inspirations.

To my brother John Pempe, who let me borrow elements of his life.

To Elizabeth Morig for her views on "the laughing Jesus."

To Juliet Waldron for sharing the poem about the Pleiades by Robert Graves.

To hearty beta readers who provided a needed boost of encouragement and improved the first draft with their suggestions: Malve Burns, Elizabeth Morig, John Pempe, Kathleen Sweeney, and Juliet Waldron.

To the Sedro-Woolley Historical Museum, its exhibits, its website, and its book *Images of America: Sedro-Woolley Washington* (2003, Arcadia) and M.J. McGoffin's book *Under the Red Roof: One Hundred Years at Northern State Hospital* (2011, McGoffin)

RUTA SEVO INFO

Novels (available on amazon.com):

Vilnius Diary (2011)

White Bird (2014)

My Boat Is So Small (2017)

Website and blog:
https://momox.org

Bio:

Sevo is a boomer, a woman of the sixties. Her fiction probably involves foreign travel, spirituality, the conventions of love, and finding yourself.

PHOTO CREDITS

Rights to photos found on dreamstime.com were purchased individually.